"Go Home Before You Get Into More Trouble Than You Can Handle."

"You once told me that you wanted a woman," Melody purred. "Not a girl."

Her voice, those eyes, everything she did... All of a sudden North was panting.

"Well, I—I'm here now...."

"It's too late," North muttered thickly.

"What if *I* want to be your woman?"

"Go home."

"But I sent the cab away."

"I'll drive you."

Her gaze locked with his. "I've got a better idea. Let me prove I'm all grown up."

She seemed so young and eager, so fragile, so beautiful. "Come here," he whispered....

Dear Reader,

Welcome to the world of Silhouette Desire, where you can indulge yourself every month with romances that can only be described as passionate, powerful and provocative!

The ever-fabulous Ann Major offers a *Cowboy Fantasy,* July's MAN OF THE MONTH. Will a fateful reunion between a Texas cowboy and his ex-flame rekindle their fiery passion? In *Cherokee,* Sheri WhiteFeather writes a compelling story about a Native American hero who, while searching for his Cherokee heritage, falls in love with a heroine who has turned away from hers.

The popular miniseries BACHELOR BATTALION by Maureen Child marches on with *His Baby!*—a marine hero returns from an assignment to discover he's a father. The tantalizing Desire miniseries FORTUNES OF TEXAS: THE LOST HEIRS continues with *The Pregnant Heiress* by Eileen Wilks, whose pregnant heroine falls in love with the investigator protecting her from a stalker.

Alexandra Sellers has written an enchanting trilogy, SONS OF THE DESERT: THE SULTANS, launching this month with *The Sultan's Heir.* A prince must watch over the secret child heir to the kingdom along with the child's beautiful mother. And don't miss Bronwyn Jameson's Desire debut—an intriguing tale involving a self-made man who's *In Bed with the Boss's Daughter.*

Treat yourself to all six of these heart-melting tales of Desire—and see inside for details on how to enter our Silhouette Makes You a Star contest.

Enjoy!

Joan Marlow Golan

Joan Marlow Golan
Senior Editor, Silhouette Desire

Please address questions and book requests to:
Silhouette Reader Service
U.S.: 3010 Walden Ave., P.O. Box 1325, Buffalo, NY 14269
Canadian: P.O. Box 609, Fort Erie, Ont. L2A 5X3

Cowboy Fantasy
ANN MAJOR

Published by Silhouette Books
America's Publisher of Contemporary Romance

I dedicate this story to my darling mother, the "real"
ANN MAJOR. Nobody ever had a sweeter mother.

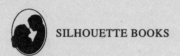 SILHOUETTE BOOKS

ISBN 0-373-76375-1

COWBOY FANTASY

Copyright © 2001 by Ann Major

Books by Ann Major

ANN MAJOR

loves writing romance novels as much as she loves reading them. She is a proud mother of three grown children. She lists hiking in the Colorado mountains with her husband, playing tennis, sailing, enjoying her cats and playing the piano among her favorite activities.

SILHOUETTE MAKES YOU A STAR!
Feel like a star with Silhouette.
Look for the exciting details of our new contest
inside all of these fabulous Silhouette novels:

Romance

 #1528 His Secret Heir
Elizabeth Harbison

 #1529 Crazy for Lovin' You
Teresa Southwick

#1530 Travis Comes Home
Patricia Thayer

#1531 Tick Tock Goes the Baby Clock
Julianna Morris

 #1532 Husband by Inheritance
Cara Colter

#1533 A Saddle Made for Two
Roxann Delaney

Special Edition

#1405 Single with Twins
Joan Elliott Pickart

 #1406 The McCaffertys: Matt
Lisa Jackson

#1407 Handprints
Myrna Temte

 #1408 When I See Your Face
Laurie Paige

 #1409 Match Made in Wyoming
Patricia McLinn

#1410 The Child She Always Wanted
Jennifer Mikels

Desire

 #1375 Cowboy Fantasy
Ann Major

#1376 Cherokee
Sheri WhiteFeather

 #1377 His Baby!
Maureen Child

 #1378 The Pregnant Heiress
Eileen Wilks

 #1379 The Sultan's Heir
Alexandra Sellers

#1380 In Bed with the Boss's Daughter
Bronwyn Jameson

Intimate Moments

 #1087 Taylor's Temptation
Suzanne Brockmann

#1088 Born a Hero
Paula Detmer Riggs

#1089 The Seduction of Goody Two-Shoes
Kathleen Creighton

#1090 Out of Nowhere
Beverly Bird

#1091 Protector with a Past
Harper Allen

#1092 Twice Upon a Time
Jennifer Wagner

Prologue

─────

South Texas
The borderlands

Black feathers spun lazily above in a cloudless, azure sky.

Teo's head hurt as he lay on the hard earth watching the big black birds. His stomach throbbed queasily.

He didn't know where he was, only that he was somewhere north of the border, somewhere in *Tejas*. Somewhere on a huge ranch the *coyote* had called El Dorado.

Teofilo Perez was ten years old and he was dying.

"Mamacíta!"

Teofilo's hands clawed sand. Then he remembered.

She'd sent him off to scavenge another part of *el dompe* with Chaco and his gang. Then she and Papacíto had run away.

When Teo had stayed up all night waiting for them, Chaco had laughed.

"They aren't coming back. It happens all the time. *Todo el tiempo.*" Chaco had stared indifferently toward the north. "There are many orphans in *el dompe*. Left behind when their families disappear over the wire. My father...too."

Now Chaco was gone as well.

Sweat stung Teo's eyes like hot tears. Where was he?

Burrs and thorns bit into his back. Here there were snakes and spiders in the high grasses; wild animals, too. If Teo didn't get up and go on, he'd die.

Then it would all be for nothing.

He was burning up, from the inside out; starving, too. He felt as thirsty for water as a bone-dry sponge. Then the coyotes started howling again, and he tasted the coppery flavor of his own panic.

He had to get up and catch Chaco. He had to keep walking north through the endless sandy pastures choked with mesquite and huisache that led to *el norte*.

To Houston. To Tiá Irma.

Chaco had warned him to stay out of the open, so *La Migra* couldn't spot him from their helicopters.

Teo felt too weak to stand, so he lay on the hard, packed ground, his swollen, sunburned lids blinking, his eyes blurring every time he opened them. Through the screen of his dense lashes a too-bright sun spun above the stunted oak trees, shooting diamond-patterned pricks through the branches. The orange orb grew bigger and bigger until it exploded in a blinding brilliance that flooded the white-heat of that harsh, unforgiving sky.

His last meal had been breakfast two days ago—two boiled eggs and three tortillas that had been gritty and stale. His hands fisted again; he tried to swallow, but his tongue was too swollen and his throat too raw and gritty.

Fat black flies buzzed. Some mysterious creature grunted and snorted in the thicket. Teo shivered as he imagined the claws of a puma or the teeth of a coyote.

"Ayudame, Dios."

He wanted to go home, not to *Cartolandia,* which was *pocho* for Cardboard Land, the barrio where they'd lived near *el dompe* in Nuevo Laredo. No, he wanted to go back home to his mountainous village, Tepóztlan. But there were no jobs there for Papacíto, no future for any of them. Nothing.

Nada, nada, mi hijo.

Papacíto had said those same words a week ago after government tractors and bulldozers had crushed their shack and bedraggled garden along with thousands of others and left them homeless again.

The next day, Papacíto had run away. Probably to look for work in *el norte.*

Teo couldn't remember the last time he'd been in school or even his last bath. He felt like a slab of meat drying in the sun, a worn-out corpse.

Papacíto had promised him a house in *el norte* with a flush toilet, toys, a garden where he could play.

Swish. Black feathers were falling out of the sky, crash-landing clumsily, settling themselves in the branches of the thorny thicket.

Vultures.

Teo stared stupidly at the big black bird folding his wings. Another bird hopped out of a tree and scuttled closer.

Teo had to get up, but when he struggled to his knees, he reeled dizzily. Once he had crawled on bleeding knees to pray to the Virgin in Mexico City. That memory was followed by a sweeter one. He was home in the cool shade of his porch, lying on his hammock, and his mother and grandmother were singing him a lullaby. He began whispering his Hail Marys.

When he opened his eyes again, he was on the ground, and the buzzards were circling lazily against the pale blue. Through swirls of dust, a lone rider on a big black horse moved toward him. The tall man, whose low-crowned sombrero was the color of dust, wore a strange costume of weathered rawhide. He was as filthy as Teo, yet he sat on his horse with a world-weary cockiness that said he was somebody, more than border trash from *el dompe*.

Although the man's coppery face was hard and lean, his teeth were as white as the *chicles* Teo had sold to the fat gringo *turistas*. He had a golden mustache.

Terrified, Teo grabbed at his plastic bag of tortillas that Chaco had tied to his belt. In his other hand he gripped the bottle that held the remains of Chaco's red soft drink. Swaying weakly, drowning in the blinding sunlight, Teo struggled to his feet.

The man called down to him gently in his native tongue, more gently than Papacíto ever spoke. *"Cuidado, manito."*

Was he a phantom? A trick, like the trick the *coyote* had played when he'd dumped Chaco and the other toughs from *el dompe* here, in the middle of nowhere, swearing that a truck would be waiting for them a little farther where the pasture hit the road past the immigration checkpoint.

The stranger's manner and the fact that he spoke a lilting, peculiarly accented Spanish was more terrifying than anything.

Then he saw her.

The trees began to whirl, and Teo was on the ground again, his dirty white shirt covered in blood. Only it wasn't blood. It was the sugary soft drink. He'd spilled the last of Chaco's precious drink.

Chaco would beat him for sure. Sobbing, he begged God to tell Chaco he was sorry, to tell his mother he was sorry he hadn't minded when she'd told him to sweep the street or bring her a bucket of water.

When the tall dusty rider got off his horse, Teo screamed and screamed.

Until he saw a girl running lightly beside the huge man. Her hair was straight and reddish gold, with deep shifting highlights glinting in the hot blaze of light that flowed all around her.

She was an angel.

His very own angel.

Teo closed his eyes, and a great peace stole over him. He wasn't afraid to die anymore.

"Angelita!" he whispered.

He opened his eyes. The girl wasn't an angel. It was his mother, and her voice was as sweet as those songs she used to sing before he went to sleep.

"Don't be afraid. You are safe, little one."

With the last of his strength, Teo stretched his thin hand toward her, but she vanished.

There was only the mysterious rider.

Only terror.

Only death in a strange, wild land.

One

South Texas
El Dorado Ranch

A bad woman can ruin the best man alive, same as a bad man can destroy a good woman.

El Dorado Ranch, set as it was right square in the borderlands cactus country of the biggest state in the continental union, might seem too rough a place for sob-sister tales to get a firm hold. But there's nothing more fascinating than love gone wrong; nothing more fun to talk about, either—especially if it's the boss's love life gone wrong.

North Black, for all that his daddy had been a local legend, for all that North had inherited his own natural arrogance and aura of cowboy majesty, for all that he sat that high-steppin', champion quarter horse, which had set him back a cool half million, for all that his carved leather saddle was trimmed in sterling, for all that he'd been billed by the state's most popular magazine as the most eligible bachelor in Texas—for all *that,* this cowboy king was damned near done for.

Nothing is more disagreeable or more difficult to stop than gossip, especially when it's true. It was common knowledge at El Dorado Ranch—better known, at least in these parts, as North Black's private kingdom—that the king was on the verge of collapse. And not only because the worst drought in living memory plagued his vast ranch in south Texas. But because an impossible little spitfire had gotten a grip on his heart and then done him wrong.

North was killing himself with overwork, his loyal crew said, doing way more than his share of the real cowboying. Why, the king was up before dawn and working cattle long after dark. Even when his hands quit, he never took a break. His lunch was a sandwich in the saddle topped off with a swig out of his canteen. Evenings, when no serious rustling or poaching mischief was afoot, were spent in his office poring over ledgers or talking on the phone.

Wherever there was trouble—illegals, bulls loose, broken pipes, cut fences, dry water holes, cows lost, a horse that needed to be broken, or more of the Midnight Bandit's mischief, North took the job on himself. Then there was Gran, who stole his best cowboys to work her garden every time he turned his back.

Nobody blamed North for wanting to work himself to death. Not after what that little witch, Melody Woods, had done to him—time and again.

First, she'd jilted him at the altar like he was a nobody—right there, in front of God, his crew, his friends, his family; hell, in front of the entire damned ranching aristocracy of Texas. She'd made a fool of him, the king, a man known to be too arrogant and too proud.

"She did worse than hurt his pride," said Sissy, his wild sister, who was worrying about him more than usual. "She broke his heart." And Sissy knew a thing or two about broken hearts.

"His father would never have lost it over a woman," Libby Black, his grandmother asserted at every possible occasion. "The ranch came first."

"You always make El Dorado sound like a religion, Gran," Sissy said.

"It was till I got some sense and took up gardening."

"It's not a religion," Sissy said. "Not for me."

"Which is why I put North in charge."

Not that North ever talked about the impossible Miss Woods. Not even after he'd fallen for her sister, Claire, on the rebound. Fortunately he and Claire had come to their senses, realizing they should be friends rather than lovers.

Gossip had it that Miss Melody Woods had had a hand in the breakup of that romance. That very same night, first chance she got, she'd gone and made a fool of him again.

Yes, sirree. She'd turned the king into a jealousy-crazed maniac in a run-down bar in Rockport, Texas. Hell, that shrimpers' dive better known as Shorty's, was so bad, the king would never have set the scuffed toe of his handmade, black boot inside it, if Melody hadn't lured him there on purpose. For reasons known only to her, she'd danced and gotten those rough, dangerous fishermen in such a rowdy stir, they would've given her more than she'd bargained for, if the king hadn't rushed her and carried her off over his shoulders like he was a caveman and she was his woman.

Only she wasn't his woman or ever going to be—according to him. The hands knew that because the very next day a couple of greenhorns at El Dorado were stupid enough to make crude bets as to exactly what the king must've done to punish Miss Woods in bed later that night. When Lester Rivers got himself liquored up enough to ask the king, who was even taller and broader-shouldered than Lester, for details about their little romp, it had taken Jeff Gentry, his burly foreman and best friend, and W.T., the laziest cowboy on El Dorado, to hold North long enough for Lester to hightail it to Laredo.

Later, the king had thanked everybody, even W.T., for saving him from strangling Lester with his bare hands. Then North had said, very softly, very calmly, but in *that* voice, everybody in his kingdom, even Gran, understood.

"What happened *that* night is nobody's business but mine! Nobody, none of you, is to ever even think about what Melody Woods does in or out of my bed or ever say her name at El Dorado Ranch again! As far as I'm concerned, she no longer exists. Understand? *Comprende?*"

Nobody had spoken of her, in Spanish or English—at least, not directly and not within the king's earshot. But the forbidden holds a mighty powerful appeal. Especially for comrades in a cow camp lonely for female companionship, especially when that forbidden female is willowy and sexy and full of surprises as a brand-new kitten.

It was plain to see by the stubborn set of North's strong, jutting jaw, he wasn't over *that* night. Plain to see by his stern silences and his inability to even crack a smile at his men's dirty banter, that the king hadn't forgotten the young lady or that night any more than they had.

No, sirree. The king wasn't through with Miss Melody Woods.

Any more than that little firecracker was through with him.

It was just a matter of time before that pair got into a tussle again.

What would that sexy little gal dream up for an encore?

His men's yelps along with that damn cow's stomping and grunting and snorting inside the jug at the far end of the huge barn would have set a sane man's nerves on edge. North was hardly sane.

He hadn't been himself since that night when Melody had danced for the world and then refused to dance with him in private. To make matters worse, Dee Dee Woods, Melody's socially ambitious mom, had him on the phone

and was unraveling the fraying ends of his frazzled psyche
with her shrill demands.

"I said supper!"

He held the phone away from his ear. How could such
a pretty woman have such a grating voice? "Tonight? Your
house? I don't think that's a good—"

"But Melody's safe and sound in Austin."

He knew better than to argue.

"Sam and I miss you. That's why when your accountant
said you were coming to town, I decided to call."

He missed them, too. "Just a second, Dee Dee. We've
got a cow in labor, and Jeff's yelling so loud—"

On a shudder, North pressed the cordless telephone
tighter against his ear and bolted himself inside the stall
with his pet llamas. Camels, he called them when he was
feeling affectionate or worried, which was all the time, ever
since Little Camel had been born so puny.

Not that it was any quieter inside their stall. Not with
that distressed cow in labor, bawling and fit to be tied again.

"What was that you said, Dee Dee?" North demanded.

He liked Dee Dee Woods even if she'd set her sights on
him as a future son-in-law for all the wrong reasons.

"I heard you'd be in town," Dee Dee shrieked. "So, I
called to invite you to supper."

The cow started kicking so loud North could barely hear
her.

"It'll just be Sam and me...I promise!"

"All right."

"Seven-thirty sharp."

He said bye and hung up.

"Boys," he shouted. "I was on the phone. Y'all were
hollering so loud, I couldn't hear myself think. I just did a
very stupid thing."

"W.T. let go, and she kicked me—two hooves, square
in the chest!" Jeff yelled back at him. "Get down here,
King!"

North was so mad he stayed put.

Damn it. It was Jeff's fault he'd said yes to Dee Dee Woods. Gentry deserved to sweat. Hell, droplets of the stuff were trickling from North's wet black hair, soaking his denim shirt and blue surgical overalls as he considered sitting down to dinner in the Woodses' house again.

He'd said yes.

Not to worry. You have a date with Maria on Saturday. You're through with Melody.

Just talking to *her* mother had brought everything back, especially *that* night.

North stood alone in a stall, occupied not by a cow or horse, but by that unlikely pair of camels and wondered if he should call Dee Dee back and send his regrets.

He began to frown in earnest as he stroked the mama llama. Then he eyed her gangly newborn more worriedly. The mother was dark brown with black patches on her face and rump. Her milk wouldn't come, and the baby—an impossibly skinny runt who was all ribs and neck and matchstick legs—couldn't suckle.

For some foolish reason, even after nights spent chasing the Midnight Bandit, North had been getting to the barn at 4:00 a.m. to play nursemaid to the shy baby llama, warming bottles, cradling him, feeding him. Even so, Little Camel wasn't putting on weight.

Jeff yelled, "Time to play vet, King."

"See you later, Little Camel," North whispered with more affection than he wanted to feel.

The shy, scared baby reminded him of...

He saw a little girl on the ground, her skirts hiked, her skinny knees torn and bloody; worse, her smoky-blue eyes dark with fear. Abruptly the king stopped that memory.

His defiant boot heels echoing all the way to the rafters, North stalked across the concrete floor of his barn toward the scuffle of his men and the cow in that distant stall.

It was late August and 113 degrees in the shade outside if it was a degree. Inside the barn felt like a sauna. He

could almost feel the beige dust that coated his wavy hair
and dark skin turn to mud and ooze under his collar.

North was exhausted, on edge, but he forced himself to
concentrate on the job ahead instead of on…on Melody.

Damn her hide…or rather her silky, golden skin. And
she was soft—he'd never forget how good she'd felt the
first time he'd accidentally touched her and she'd jumped
as if she'd been shot. Not that every nerve in his body
hadn't popped like sparklers, too.

Why the hell had Dee Dee called? He didn't want Melody on his mind. For months he'd refused to think about
her.

He didn't still want her, still dream about her. He didn't.
Not after what she'd done. Not after what she hadn't done.

But if some idiotic part of him still did want her, that
was the part he was trying damned hard to kill by working
himself so hard. His misplaced affection for the wrong
woman had jeopardized not only his pride and his heart,
but also his family and their ranch.

He had a position to uphold. When he married, if he
married after what she'd put him through, it would be to a
mature, sensible woman who understood ranching, who
could contribute something of value to El Dorado, who
would lend sanity to his hard life instead of chaos, who
could make commitments and stick to them. He wanted a
harmonious marriage to a woman, who could show a man
she loved him in a warm womanly way, to a woman like
Maria Langly, who had been born and bred to ranch life,
just as he had.

North was fighting for his ranch, his legacy and his
world. His back was against the wall. He had no time to
waste on a woman who'd never known for sure whether
she wanted him, a woman who would never be anything
but trouble.

Unbidden came the vision of a long, cool slip of a girl
in skintight jeans and a halter top. Melody did have the
cutest and most mischievous smile and the softest honey-

red, straight hair. She smelled good, too. And, boy, when that little exhibitionist hadn't been driving him crazy, or turning him on, she sure had made him laugh. Nobody had ever been able to make him forget, at least for a little while, the ranch and the heavy responsibilities he'd assumed too young.

She was cute. Trouble was, she knew it. She'd reveled in making him forget that he was supposed to be stern and tough, that as the largest landowner in south Texas, he was supposed to set an example for his men, for the whole damn ranching community in these parts.

Hell, his granddaddy had taken him up on his saddle when he was five. They'd worked cattle together, and all the while the old man had been whispering that when he was a man, all this—meaning the cattle, the vast acreage— would be his responsibility. His father, Rand Black, had been a legend. North was determined to carry on his daddy's legacy and support the people whose families had lived here for generations, who depended on him for their very livelihoods.

Melody never bowed down and worshiped him like everybody else around here. So, why the hell had he loved this defiant brat since she'd been a young girl? She wasn't even any good in bed. She was too uptight and skittish to be sexy in private. At least with him. No, she preferred public displays of wanton affection that drove him and every other guy who caught her performance wild. Always, she left him hot and hard and frustrated, and jealous as all get out. When they were alone, and he made a move, she got as scared and shy as his baby camel. He loathed everybody thinking she was hot and easy when that's the last thing she was.

Except for that last night.

You're not supposed to think about her or what happened, ever again. You're supposed to work—till you forget her.

So, how come you accepted a dinner invitation tonight in Corpus Christi from her mother?

Because Dee Dee swore Melody's in Austin and you won't see her. Or talk about her. Because it was so hot and loud in the barn you hadn't been able to think.

Liar.

You want to see Dee Dee's most recent pictures of *her* on the fridge. You want Dee Dee to drop those annoying little hints...

Forget her!

North was trying. He'd all but imprisoned himself on his ranch. He had 800,000 acres of baking shin oak and prickly pear and thousands of head of cattle to protect him from that clueless she-devil, who had a lot of growing up to do up in Austin.

North could hear his stressed cattle outside squalling as his men cut them from the herd and drove them into pens and chutes, some to be kept and fed, some to be vaccinated and tagged, some to be loaded onto the cattle trucks that were discreetly hidden in mesquite thickets.

Tough times made for brutal decisions.

No matter how much land or money a rancher had, he was powerless against the weather and the hard realities of market prices. Due to the drought, he'd run out of grass. The beef market was flooded. The cost of feed was too high to keep the herd. Then last night the Midnight Bandit had cut his fence and tried to rustle a truckload of cows again.

Outside the barn, horses neighed and sputtered. The cattle roared, and his men shouted. These were the familiar, beloved sounds of home to North. And of doom.

For more than a hundred years this ranch had been owned and run by Blacks. The pictures of his ancestors hung inside the ranch house, their grim expressions setting standards and demanding impossibilities of him in these modern times.

Inside the stall now, North was still sweating profusely

as he picked up a scalpel, still in its wrapper. He picked up the irritated, very pregnant cow's tail, then let it drop. She didn't react.

"Looks like the spinal's okay, King," Jeff said behind him.

"Good."

Jeff was wide as a beam and nearly as tall as North; he was red-haired, bowlegged, narrow-eyed, and bullheaded. But a lady's man nonetheless. His daddy had been the ranch foreman before him, and his daddy before him. Jeff had grown up on the ranch just like North had. They were closer than most brothers. El Dorado was that kind of place.

"So, let's get to work—fast," Jeff urged.

North inspected the shaved area and the black lines Jeff had drawn along the reddish brown hide. When he was satisfied, he injected a topical anesthetic along every inch of the line. After he sliced through the hide with the scalpel, Jeff injected more anesthetic inside the incision. North began to cut deeper.

There were a lot of bleeders, but North deftly stopped them. Within a minute he was popping hooves out of the cow's belly and Jeff was pulling the rest of the calf free. They worked together, in harmony, as they always did, smiling at each other after it was over because it was a helluva rush to look into those wet brown eyes and witness the beginning of a new life.

Another life saved.

But for what? North wondered silently as he knew Jeff did. If it didn't rain? For an early death in a slaughterhouse…his short life bartered for a few peanuts? Worse, he might get himself rustled and hauled south to Mexico.

Again, North thought of Melody who'd become a vegetarian just to spite him after her first and only visit to the ranch.

North frowned as he dropped antibiotics into the uterus and then began to sew up the cow, barking questions at

Jeff to distract himself from Melody. "Calf breathing okay?"

North remembered Melody saying after he'd finished a long day at the squeeze chute, "I won't ever eat a hamburger again. I keep seeing a cute little brown-eyed calf peeping its head out of my hamburger bun and pleading for help."

He stared at the cute new calf. It galled him that Melody thought he didn't care about his animals.

"He's a cute little cuss, ain't he, King?"

Forget Melody Woods.

"Get him tagged and shot!"

Within minutes, North was done and striding out of the barn in shotgun chaps made of scarred leather. He made his way toward the cloud of dust that muted the harsh sun somewhere up above in that bluish white sky.

He pulled his bandanna up and took Mr. Jim's reins. As he rode toward the herd, Jeff and the other cowboys seemed to float in a golden haze of dust.

When North got closer, Mr. Jim shook his long red mane and neighed. His vaqueros nodded in deference, and Mr. Jim reared.

"Easy, champ," North whispered to Mr. Jim.

He flicked the reins and began shouting orders to his men in fluent Spanish right before he galloped into the herd. Then, and only then, as he cut cattle alongside his day-labor cowboys, was he able to forget the impossible Melody Woods.

Because he had to drive in to Corpus Christi, he quit earlier than he had in weeks. Before going to the house, he returned to the barn.

The calf he'd delivered was doing fine, so he made a final stop at that stall occupied by the mama llama and her pitifully skinny baby.

"Jeff," he shouted.

Jeff came running. Hell, everybody came running when the king yelled.

Everybody except...*her.*

When the baby llama forgot his shyness for the first time and moved toward him trustingly on shaky legs, North melted. He remembered a skinny little girl on the ground, drying her tears with the back of her hand before throwing herself into his arms.

"How long since my baby camel here ate?" North demanded in an oddly rough voice.

"Three hours. Want me to feed her again?"

"*Him.* No," North said, surprising himself as he strode toward the refrigerator and grabbed a bottle of fresh milk. "Warm this. I'll do it."

"You're wasting a lot of time on that runt," Jeff said as North squatted near the fragile newborn.

"I guess I'm a sucker for lost causes."

Melody had said he had no heart.

The barn phone began to ring as North cradled the llama across his knees and offered him the bottle. As the camel nibbled tentatively, W.T. banged inside the stall with the cordless. The llama shivered and stopped suckling. If anybody had the look of a dimestore cowboy, it was W.T. Scuffed high-heeled boots, wide hat, the shiftless fraud carried himself with more style than anybody on El Dorado.

"Take it easy when you come in here," North whispered testily.

"Border Patrol. Delfino's at the gate in his Dodge Ramcharger demandin' access—"

North grabbed the phone. "Delfino, you'd better be here to tell me you've got a lead on the Midnight Bandit. He damn near made off with a truck—"

"No. Some half-starved illegals. Kids. Not ten miles south of your headquarters. From our helicopter. Brush too dense to land."

"Damn," North muttered.

Tough as it was in Texas, it was tougher in Mexico. And getting tougher. *Ejidos,* small Mexican settlements, sprang up along the southern edge of El Dorado almost weekly.

The people who lived in them were unemployed. They didn't have a damned thing to do but watch the goings-on at El Dorado.

North had started wearing his Colt when he worked remote pastures of his ranch. He never knew anymore who or what he might run into on his own land. Anytime he spotted illegals, he called the Border Patrol.

Melody's voice piped up in his mind. "Americans spend more than four billion dollars a year on pet food. You know what else, Bertie? We don't spend a fourth of that on food to feed starving people in third world countries."

Bertie. That was Melody's special name for the king. If ever there was a sissy nickname—

More and more, intense, desperate men seemed to be making border crossings. Not just men these days. Women and children, who were pitifully unprepared to attack the desert.

Delfino repeated that single word, "Kids."

Ten miles. Illegals never carried much food or more than a gallon of water. In this heat, on foot, they'd be dead before they reached his headquarters.

North nodded glumly. "Keep an eye out for my bandit, you hear?"

After North hung up, the llama suckled indifferently. Still, North fed the baby camel with a vengeance till the bottle was completely empty. When he was done, he touched his brow to the furry ear. "You're not going to starve on me, Little Camel. Not if I can help it!"

When North was done, he found Jeff in the tack room. "You gonna take care of Little Camel, here, while I'm gone to Corpus?"

"Corpus?" Jeff shot him a look. "What about Saturday and Maria and me and Tina?"

"Right. Saturday. Maria." North took his sweat-stained Stetson off, raked brown fingers through his black hair, set his hat back on. "Wouldn't miss it for the world." His deep voice lacked enthusiasm.

"We'll cook 'em steaks, take 'em ridin' around on the ranch, show off the spread, impress 'em and bed 'em," Jeff reminded him. "Just like old times...before *her*."

"Right. Just like old times."

Jeff resented Melody more than anybody else on the ranch. North and he had gone to college together, double-dated together. They'd been inseparable until Melody.

"Don't you worry none about Little Camel, King."

North showered and changed into a pair of faded jeans with razor-sharp creases, a long-sleeved white shirt and his best boots—his uniform, Melody used to say. Then he stomped out to his white pickup. First thing he saw was his Colt in its holster on the seat.

He was licensed to carry. Quickly wrapping the belt around the holster, he got inside and jammed it into his glove compartment.

Once he left the ranch, the flat, familiar highway was clogged with speeding NAFTA trucks all the way to Robstown where he turned off for Corpus Christi.

The drive through flat, unremarkable countryside was so familiar it soon grew boring. Maybe that's why he noticed the bumper stickers peeling off the eighteen-wheeler in front of him. One was about beautifying Texas and the need to put a Yankee on a bus.

The other was about Humpty Dumpty being pushed.

North grinned. Melody loved bumper stickers.

Melody. He'd been thinking about her way too much. He should have canceled dinner at the Woodses'.

Too late. Dee Dee was a superb cook. Sam knew everything there was to know about football. North's own father had died young. Too young. Not that North let himself dwell on that.

Hell, his own mother certainly didn't dwell on it. She was in Europe blowing her fortune on the immense schloss of a Bavarian count she'd met in Paris.

The Woodses had always made a helluva fuss over North, a helluva lot more of a fuss than Melody or his own mother or even Gran ever had. Besides, he did have appointments with his accountant and cattle buyer in Corpus Christi. A frozen dinner in his bachelor apartment there held no appeal.

But the Woodses were *her* parents, and he was dating Maria now.

Only one date so far.

Not counting next Saturday.

An hour later, he was knocking briskly on the front door of the Woodses' two-story home, fighting to pretend he felt cool and was in control. When nobody answered, he jammed his fist on the doorbell. He turned to go when he heard lightly racing footsteps.

The door was thrown open by a slim hand with glossily white fingernails that had ridiculous little silver moons etched into them.

Little silver moons.

They sparkled, winking at him. Even before he saw the rest of *her,* the jolt of male-female awareness that shuddered down his spinal column told him to bolt.

Instead he drawled lazily, "Hello there, Melody."

Two

"Smile, Bertie boy. It's the second best thing you can do with your lips."

Something about Melody's low, Southern voice, something in the images she conjured was so damn sexy, so damn blatant. He began to dream about how good it could be if she put those lips to work.

"Naughty, naughty," she whispered, reading his mind.

"What the hell..."

"Relax. I didn't mean anything. I got that line off some bumper sticker when I was driving home today."

So, she'd been reading bumper stickers, too.

He moved closer. Big mistake. She smelled too good.

"I've got one for you, too, darlin'. Humpty Dumpty was pushed."

She laughed.

To keep from grinning back, he bit his tongue till he tasted blood.

Peeking from behind the door, Melody batted her long,

burnished lashes at him, just as she had *that* night when she'd come looking for him at his apartment. When the lash work got no visible reaction, her impish smile brightened, and she began to tease him in earnest.

His palms dampened. The smile was overkill. Her lash work had done the trick. So had the comment about what he could do with his lips.

No wonder the ambitious Dee Dee had called this morning. A mother knew when her daughter was in the mood to start something. In Dee Dee's mind he was a prize catch and a big enough dope to fall for her little girl all over again.

"What the hell are you doing home?" he demanded.

"Hi there to you, too—Bertie."

His mouth thinned. "Don't call me that unless…"

"Then, hi there, Rancher Black," she said sassily.

"North will do just fine."

"Aye. Aye." Instead of saluting, she touched her lip with a fluttery white fingertip and blew him a kiss.

Little moons sparked.

His lips actually got hot.

Hell, it *was* August.

His sneer was slow and deliberate, "So, you've come back—" Then he added, "What the hell for?"

She flinched at those secret code words, just as he did. Her beauty upset him even more. Her long, straight, reddish-gold hair framed the slender oval of her flushed face. Her golden skin was damp as if she'd just stepped from the shower. And those half-scared, flirty, smoky-blue eyes ate him alive. Why, oh why, did she have to smell of soap and perfumed bath oils?

Even without makeup, she was naturally, heart-wrenchingly beautiful, more beautiful and innocent looking and yet voluptuous than he remembered. She'd come looking for him after her little dance in Shorty's, after their wild kisses in the parking lot. No sooner had he pulled her inside his place *that* night, the night he'd wanted her so damn much, he'd felt as if he'd die if he couldn't have her.

She'd let him take her to bed. But first, she'd actually stripped for him.

"You say I only want to perform in public. Not tonight. Tonight I want to dance just for you. Do you want to dance with me?"

"I'm not the exhibitionist. I'll watch."

"You're gonna have fun. I promise." Her eyes had gleamed, teasing him, luring him.

She'd put a CD in his player, turned his lights way down and had begun to move in the velvet shadows. For a long time all she'd done was sway back and forth to the heavy beat and run her hands over her body. When he'd joined her, she'd let him grasp her by the waist, pull her close, let him put his hands wherever he wanted, let him strip her ever so slowly. She hadn't even fought him when he'd undone the buttons of her blouse, one by one. She'd danced and smiled and lured them both to their doom.

The ground rocked under him as he stood on her porch. His heart thudded.

"You look too damn good, darlin'," he whispered.

"So do you," she said in a sad, lost tone that matched his own.

Just those words, and he wanted to touch her so bad he hurt. But he remembered the dangerous place that desire had led them to so many times before, so he knotted his callused hands, slipped them into his hip pockets. He took a deep breath and a long step backward.

Instead of her usual grunge attire, she wore some sort of silky, scarlet sarong that clung to her curves so tightly, he saw nipples. And that there was no panty line. It wasn't hard to imagine her body since he knew exactly what she looked like with nothing on. Show but don't let him touch, being her motto.

"How the hell could you answer the door in that? I could've been anyone."

"It would have been a whole lot less dangerous if you had been," she teased before she realized what she was doing. "I was expecting you."

Her pupils darkened with alarm, but not before her husky voice had rippled over every raw nerve ending, making his skin sting as if he was on fire the way it had *that* night.

"But you have no right, no claim on me or what I wear...or don't wear—ever again, Rancher Black." She lifted her chin, challenging him to more verbal dueling.

"You're right, of course—Miss Woods!"

No doubt she'd purchased the improbable garment somewhere in the Orient when she'd run away from him on that freighter and driven him mad with jealousy, rage and fear. When she'd finally turned up safe and sound, she'd thrown his life into turmoil all over again when she'd almost seduced him. Then she'd gone off to India.

"I was in the shower," she said demurely without lifting her gaze to his. "My muscles were stiff after the long drive."

All of a sudden he had a stiff muscle problem and a mighty keen need for a cold shower, too.

"Would you prefer it if I'd answered the door stark naked?" she teased.

The vision of her naked in a shower stall brought a rush of heat and made the muscle in question pull even tighter. Just for an instant he remembered her in a black lace bra and matching panties and a black velvet hat after he'd removed her blouse and jeans. For no reason at all, he was tugging at his collar.

"Don't worry...Bertie. If I'd known you were going to be in such a bad mood, I wouldn't have answered the door at all."

"Why aren't you in Austin where you belong?" His voice was as cold as ice.

"Why did you say yes to my mother? This is my parents' house. It's your own fault if you're not where you belong—

out on your big ole ranch. Playing king, doing your big man things. Ordering everybody in your kingdom around.''

That wasn't how it was. Not that he let on.

"Is that what you think of me and my business?"

"Isn't that what you want everybody to think?"

"I have responsibilities."

"And they came before me."

His family hadn't thought so. "They're a part of who I am."

"And I don't know who I am. Is that what you're saying?"

In bed or out of it, he almost shouted. Instead he flushed darkly. "My ranch wasn't the problem."

"You give everything of yourself to that ranch."

"Because I have to."

"Why?"

"Because my father died that's why!" North remembered the fire. He remembered running. He remembered screaming for help.

"Why you, Bertie?"

"Just…just…" An emotion built and burst inside him, so he waited. "Just because," he finished darkly, remembering his father's funeral. "I'm his son. That's all."

Her eyes seemed to see inside him, into that shadowy secret place.

She smiled. "You can tell me."

He glared. "Can I? If you were me, would you trust you…after…"

They'd hardly said hi, and already they were at it.

Yet he preferred arguing and probably so did she—to remembering *that* night and what had happened in his apartment and what hadn't.

She was pale and yet breathing hard, every bit as agitated as he was. Those fingers with the little silver moons were tugging at her silken sash. "How can we be discussing this…like it still matters? When nothing about us matters…anymore."

He watched that rhythmic tugging of those little half

moons at her sash as if hypnotized. "My thoughts exactly, darlin'."

So why was there a painful lump in his throat? Why that painful thickening lower down that stretched his jeans and made him too conscious of her easy power? Why were the memories of his childhood all mixed up with the crazy sexual frustration of that last night? Why this insane desire to yank that infernal sash loose, slide his hands inside that silk robe and pull her against his body when he knew why wanting her was so impossible?

Why couldn't she be *normal?* Why did she have to be the sexiest woman alive and not sexy at all?

Those moving fingertips with the little moons that twinkled slid along red silk. He felt his collar tighten like it was really choking him. "Stop playing with that damned sash!"

"Sorry."

"Do I come in or go?" he growled when her slim hands were still at last. "It's been a long day."

"Oh, do come in, Rancher Black," she teased, pushing the door wider.

"Quit calling me that!"

When she didn't move out of his way, he was forced to sidle so close to her he almost brushed against her. Which was what she must have wanted because when he was almost past her, she reached out and laid her hand on his shoulder.

"North, I..." Even before the panic flared in her eyes, she chopped off the end of her sentence.

Instantly his muscles contracted beneath the liquid heat of her slim hand. His black head jerked, startling her, and for a long moment they both stared at those fingertips with the tiny silver moons. She'd scarcely touched him, but the effect on his senses was electrifying.

He remembered that last night when her hands had been all over him. She'd been eager, as eager as he. And then suddenly, she'd gotten scared.

''North...'' Her little girl voice died in her throat as she splayed her fingers, causing the tiny little moons to twinkle.

He felt her, remembered her in every pore. They'd lain in his bed that night, his body pressed firmly against hers, her lips against his throat, her breast against his chest, the rest of their bodies touching all the way down. She'd felt so right. She always did.

He'd held her for a long time, stroking her hair, trying to gentle her as he might a frightened colt. But she'd gotten frightened again and gone back to the wild on him anyway.

''Don't start in on me again, darlin'...unless you intend to finish what you start...this time.''

Her hand tightened and then fell away slowly, and still he couldn't move past her any more than she seemed able to escape him.

''I want to forget you,'' he said, but his gaze was on her pink lips.

''That does seem like the sensible solution to our problem.''

''*Your* problem,'' he said in a flat tone.

''And yet—''

''There is not going to be a yet—damn you.''

She blushed. Her eyes remained downcast. ''What if I can't be as sensible or as rational as you? What if I—''

''Not if you crawled—''

She went white at that code word.

''You broke up with me, remember?'' he said in a softer tone.

''And you'll never be able to forgive—'' Her husky voice had dropped, too—to something that sounded close to shame or regret.

''That's right.''

Leave her alone. Cool off. Talk football outside with Sam.

But she looked so small and vulnerable. Suddenly he couldn't stop staring at her lips and wondering how long since anybody had kissed their wet, pink fullness. Wondering who else knew how they tasted. These thoughts got him so riled, North pushed his way inside, grabbed her, backed her against the red flowers on the foyer wallpaper and pressed his body firmly against hers.

She swallowed. Her eyes shone nervously; her cheeks blazed a brighter hue, but for once, she didn't try to run.

Suddenly his breathing was fast and irregular. "Why? Why do you always goad me? Why do you always have to push?"

"I—I don't know. I-it's just the way I am with you. I don't like it that I do it, either. North—"

"Shut up," he said silkily.

Then he touched her cheek with the back of his hand, ran it along her throat. Her skin was smooth and soft. Womanly soft. And hot. So hot. She was burning up just like he was.

"Let me go," she whispered.

He stroked her hair. "Not just yet. You touched me. You led me on."

"You're too easy."

He grinned. "If only you were as easy."

She shut her eyes as if to shut him out.

"Your desires are every bit as deep and dark as mine," he murmured. "Have you found someone else to satisfy them?" Just asking her drove him crazy.

Her lashes fluttered. Her smoky eyes darkened. "No…"

"How long…since you've been held? Kissed?"

"Not since…that night." She turned deep red.

"Me, either."

Why the hell had he admitted that? Unwanted desire for her wound him tighter. When she tried to run, he seized her arm again. "Not yet, darlin'. You're not going anywhere. Not just yet. Not till I've had a final taste."

Melody was tall, but he dwarfed her. Easily he scooped her closer. When he snugged her hips against his, she quivered, and even the slight response on her part that warred with the wild panic in her eyes made him explosively needy. Always, always she drove him past the limits of his careful control.

"Why do you always bully me?" she whispered.

"Sometimes I think because you want me to."

"Don't say that."

"What do you want, Melody? What's so wrong—"

An electric silence hummed between them. She was nervy, yet secretly thrilled and eager, too.

"You scare me," she said breathily.

"You scare you. You ought to know by now I would never hurt you. Or force you—"

"That's exactly what you're doing."

"I just want to touch you." He wanted to slide his fingers inside her again, to know she was wet as she'd been that night, despite all her puritanical and hung-up assertions to the contrary.

She shut her eyes, half opened her mouth and sank back against the wall. "If only—"

God, it had been so long. Six months since that wonderful, awful night. He had told himself, never, ever again—not with her. Then the minute he set eyes on her, the minute she touched him, she had him again. More than anything he craved to kiss her, to run his hands through her long, soft hair, to do all the things she'd forbidden him to do.

What would she do this time if he tried? What would she say? What would he do if she ever let him? He'd wanted her so damn much. He'd waited so long.

Maybe he would have held himself in check if Melody hadn't reached up and brushed her fingertips against the crisp black hair above his white collar. Maybe. But even though her touch was light and tentative, he felt her feverish response behind it, and that alone set him off.

He seized her shoulders to pull her toward him, wondering if this time she'd—

His head came down. Her lips pursed eagerly as she lifted them. In the fraction of a second before their mouths touched, he thought she whispered, "I'm sorry, North. So, sorry."

But before he could deepen their kiss, he heard the brisk patter of Dee Dee's footsteps. Quickly he straightened, and Melody twisted her crimson face away, so her mother couldn't read her.

"Is that you, North!" Dee Dee shrieked from the other end of the hall as she rushed down the hall that was papered to look like a voluptuous garden gone wild in spring.

He froze.

Melody jumped free and began smoothing her hair.

"North...Melody..."

Dee Dee, who was golden and gorgeous and looked years younger than she was, smiled as they hastily backed away from each other and began to fidget—Melody with her sash after she'd finished on her hair and he with his tight collar.

"It's so good to see you, dear." Dee Dee smiled knowingly as she came forward and stretched on tiptoes as if to peck his dark cheek. All he felt when her glossy lips hovered close was the stir of her warm breath against his skin. "I'm the chairman of the charity ball, so I was on the phone and couldn't get the door."

"You said Melody was in Austin."

"Did I?" Dee Dee smiled up at him artlessly. "You know Melody. She's as fickle as Texas weather, and I suppose we're about due for a norther."

"After this hellish summer, something a little cool...and frosty might be a welcome change," he agreed thickly, his eyes on Melody.

"Sam's out back," Dee Dee said. When an alarm buzzed in her kitchen, she started. "Why don't you join him, dear? And while you're outside, make sure he doesn't burn up my rib eyes. Meanwhile, I'll go get you a beer out of the fridge.'' Then she flew to the kitchen to check on whatever she had in the oven.

"It's only one evening together," North muttered in a hoarse whisper to Melody. "Surely we can be civil and behave ourselves in front of your parents for a few hours— for their sake. For ours, too.''

"Only one night?" Melody looked a little strained as she smiled up at him. "Oh, no, North. I quit my job. I'm home to stay. Or at least I'll be at Nana's. You and I could see each other anytime—that is, if we wanted to.''

"Which we don't.''

"Speak for yourself. The last thing I intend to do where you're concerned—is behave myself.''

Nana was her grandmother.

"I thought south Texas bored you.''

"I was wrong…about a lot of things.''

He remembered her apology right before their kiss. "What things? What do you mean?''

"I'll be around. That's all.''

"You said you loved Austin because it was wild. That south Texas and I bored—''

Her parting shots had cut him to the quick. At one point she'd said he was so ultraconservative that she felt stifled and dead anytime she was anywhere near him.

"Well—'' She paused. "I'm here for a while. Not because of you, but because I'm going back to school. To get a masters and a teaching certificate.''

"Teaching? You said you didn't want to settle for any sort of traditional roles like wife or teacher that women used to be forced into by macho men.''

"I was a child. Naturally I wanted to be glamorous and special.'' She paused. "I guess I figured out I like kids. I figured out some other stuff…that I like, too.''

Like men? Like sex? *Like me?*

As if she read his mind, Melody notched her chin upward a bit defiantly, and he found himself drinking in the beauty of her long slender neck and wondering if she really might be referring to sex.

"With this degree and certificate," Melody continued, "I can work anywhere in the world. I'll be independent."

So that was it! She hadn't come back because of him. This was about her infernal determination to be independent of him. To stay single.

Not that he cared.

"So you still want to travel?" he whispered, making his voice both insolent and admiring. "To see the world?"

"To be free," she agreed, but her tone was low and urgent as if this really was important to her, as if making him understand mattered.

"Sexually free?"

She turned red again. "Is that all you ever think about?"

"That does seem to be a burning issue when you're around."

"Which is why I wanted to get as far away from you as I possibly could!"

"To have more of your little adventures?"

Her eyes blazed. "You don't get me at all. I should've known better than to try to talk to you. You wouldn't understand."

He understood, all right. She teased him. Did she want real adventures with other, wilder men, who weren't so predictable, who didn't bore her—as he did?

"You might get into trouble. I worry about you."

"Well, don't." Her eyes smoldered. "This isn't about you, North."

Something cold coiled around his heart, and then he saw that she was trembling.

"You're right, of course," he forced himself to agree. "We broke up. Or rather, you broke up with me. You said we're—"

"Finished. And you said—" Her voice was tight and sad, and he realized his parting shots had hurt her, too.

He'd said she was doing him a favor.

She was right. They were finished. It was what she'd
wanted, what he wanted, too. He was a rancher, born and
bred—traditional to the core. He couldn't change that. He
couldn't—not for her, not after everything she'd done.

Even so, the thought of other men touching her...of her
touching them...

That shouldn't have bothered him. But his stomach
twisted, and a bleak, lonely wave of despair washed over
him as he considered working his ranch, dating other
women, even Maria—while Melody had romantic adventures.

"I—I guess I'll go and get dressed," she said after an
awkward spell.

When she left him, North's gaze followed her. Her waist
was slim, the flare of her hips and thighs enticingly sweet.
That short red silk thing made her look leggy and coltish.
He couldn't seem to move till she disappeared from his
view.

Then he adjusted his collar and raked his hand through
his hair. So what if he had to endure one miserable night
with her?

They'd catch up on old times. Then he really would forget her. He'd see Maria on Saturday, and maybe he'd find
a bad girl on the side to sleep with. From now on, he'd
drown himself in other women instead of work.

The only reason Miss Melody Woods was getting to him
tonight was that she'd burned him so bad, he'd avoided all
women since her.

Until Maria, he reminded himself. Maria was perfect for
him. At least Jeff said so.

Could he help it if Melody looked good enough to eat,
and that he was starved?

One night with her.

What could possibly go wrong?

*Smile. It's the second best thing you can do with your
lips.*

Why did those infernal words keep repeating themselves

like a broken record? Why did he keep imagining her mouth on his body?

He didn't like the heat those images brought.

One night.

That was all.

Three

___

Vegetarian alert: Take a flying leap!
—The Plants

The bumper sticker tacked to her mirror was the first thing Melody saw when she raced into her room. North had given it to her as a joke after she'd become a vegetarian. She'd kept it, even when he'd dated Claire. Just like she'd kept all her pictures of him, those framed and those not, at the bottom of her underwear drawer.

She was shaking as she studied the skimpy red, one-piece bathing suit she'd grabbed from her mother's drawer, shaking when she thought of wearing it outside with North there.

She shut her bedroom door and sank against it. For a second the wood felt cool against her hot skin after her steamy backyard.

After North.

Uncertain, conflicted, she threw the suit on the floor. She hated red, more than any color in the world, hated the sexy style cut high over the thigh her mother had chosen. And yet...

Mother had said it was so hot, that they should swim before supper. When Melody had mentioned she hadn't unpacked and didn't know where her suit was, Dee Dee had said, "I have a brand-new one in my top drawer you can borrow."

Stripping off her T-shirt and shorts, Melody moved past the piles of suitcases and boxes toward her flamboyantly red flowered bed, only to be upset not by her mother's gaudy decorating, but by her own reflection in the long mirror beneath the bumper sticker.

The frightened girl with those rosy cheeks in the push-up black bra and thong panties reminded her of that other queasy girl she'd seen in North's apartment mirror six months ago when she'd been trapped between boundless love and desire and sexual despair.

She'd called him an animal.

His hand had been inside her when he'd muttered, "An animal? I love you, Melody. This is what men and women who love each other do together—in private. Someday, you're going to grow up. You'll come running home, for this, darlin', but I won't be here waiting. I'm sick and tired of waiting."

Then he'd let her go and had lain on the bed beside her for a while, staring up at his ceiling fan that had spun lazily above them. Finally, when they'd both recovered a little, he'd balled her black lace panties and bra in his brown fist and thrown them at her, saying she'd come back, begging for more of the same. Saying that even if she crawled, he'd tell her he was done with a tease like her for good.

"I'm sorry," he'd said after he'd dressed, apologizing for what he'd done to her in bed and for some of what he'd said.

"I'm sorry, too."

From the door he'd lashed her with rough words that had smashed her heart. "I'm sorry I ever met you." He hadn't slammed the door. It had clicked so softly; she'd barely heard him leave. Still, a cold chill had run down her spine at the utter finality of his retreating footsteps.

Desolation had overpowered her just as fear had gotten a grip on her when he'd started making love to her, and she'd just felt so scared and helpless and had wanted to get away.

She hadn't been able to face her true feelings that night much less try to tell him. But over time, when he hadn't called, she'd begun to miss him terribly. Some inner resilience had lessened her sense of shame and intensified all the other inexplicable needs that had made her unable to forget North.

He'd been so wonderful to her in so many ways. So kind and patient, especially in those early years. But he was a man, and he needed a woman.

"I want a grown-up woman, a real woman, who knows how to love."

"You mean you want sex."

"Now that you mention it—yes. That would be a great start."

And here she was, home again, and more confused than ever about everything, including North.

North hadn't said, "I told you so," tonight.

Not in so many words. But he'd made her feel it—in every cell of her being. Every time he'd looked at her so coldly, and she'd flamed to life again, she'd remembered that night when she'd enflamed him, enticed him, and then gotten terrified, and hurt him all over again.

Melody opened her closet to search her built-in drawers for another suit. In the second drawer she found a stack of videocassette tapes. Blushing, remembering where she'd found them and what they were of, she fisted her hands like a defiant child. Then she slammed the drawer.

How could her parents watch those things? Sex? Why was it so important to everybody except her?

She'd made her choices. Why, oh why, did they have to be so hard to live with? Why, oh why, did she have to be the only modern girl in all of the United States who had hang-ups about sex?

"Get over it," Cathy, her best friend would say. "You know what they say, practice makes perfect."

North's cockiness and blatant sexiness along with Melody's natural wariness weren't going to get her down tonight. Neither was his cool, calculated indifference. Tonight would be short and sweet, like they'd agreed. Then they'd go their separate ways.

Tonight wasn't going to be about sex!

She picked up the red suit and pulled it on. When she saw herself, she gasped at how much of her backside was hanging out.

Through her gauzy curtains, she could see North and her father talking amiably, more amiably than when she'd been out there with them. She was too far away to hear the rumble of his deep drawl, too far for it to send shivers through her, but it was all too obvious, North was much more relaxed when she wasn't around.

Likewise.

He lounged against the garage, his arms crossed, his long legs sprawled apart, laughing at something her father said. When she'd been out there, too, he'd stood stiffly by her father's side, his eyes on the shrimp appetizers sizzling on the grill, his answers to her father's questions brief and uninformative when Sam had done his best to ask intelligent questions about the ranch or roundup and the drought.

Sam had watched them both as he'd taken a lengthy pull of his imported beer. "Long, hot summer?"

"Yes."

"Bad for ranching?"

North had nodded.

For the first time Melody had noticed the dark circles

under his eyes, the weariness behind his smiles. He'd been working too hard she could tell.

"Any chance of rain?" her father had asked.

"Not unless we get a hurricane."

"It rained out west last night."

Then Melody had asked, "What do you hear from your mother, North?"

"Not much."

"Do you miss her?"

"What the hell kind of question is that?" he'd snapped.

North, who had been so dark and intense in the foyer, hadn't even looked up from the grill when she'd joined them there or when she'd spoken. Not even when he'd burst out at her so angrily. His refusal to do so had gotten her even more dizzily nervous than she'd been in the foyer when he'd pinned her against the wall.

First, he'd been all over her in the foyer. Then in the backyard, not only hadn't she existed, she'd been the last person he intended to confide in.

But he'd come over, and he made her feel alive, as she hadn't in months. More alive than in India or any other exotic locale.

In the six months since *that* night, she'd gone to India and Manhattan and Boston and then back to Texas. She'd moved into a tiny cottage with an older woman named Elizabeth, who was a musician in the Austin music scene. Elizabeth did gigs almost every night. Home alone, Melody had realized she was lonelier than she ever had been in her whole life. Even so, after North she hadn't wanted to date.

She'd gotten up every morning, flossed and brushed her teeth, washed her hair and gone out to her menial job at the park. Her parents hadn't understood her not getting a "real" job, not using her education. But she'd preferred wandering through the park, being out with nature, even picking up garbage, to a real adult job.

Nights, she'd showered and gotten into bed—alone again. Her life had been a dull routine until that day Randy

Hunter, a guy she intensely disliked from school in Corpus Christi, had shown up at the park.

He'd leaned against the door of her tiny tollbooth, trapping her inside. "You look awful good in those short shorts, sugar." His hot eyes had lingered on her legs long after she'd handed him his receipt and change.

"What is that getup, a little rangerette costume?"

"I'm a park tech."

"Aren't you the girl that used to wear red panties in elementary school?"

She hadn't answered.

"What color are you wearing under—"

Shaking, she'd closed her eyes in mute panic. "Why don't you go enjoy the park."

"You still like sexy underwear?"

Randy had come to the park too often after that. But what had really bothered her was the package somebody had sent her later the same week. When she'd opened it and a pair of red thong panties had spilled out of it, she'd quit on the spot.

And come running home.

To North.

No. No. But, when Melody lifted her gauzy curtain and caught another glimpse of North, her heart started hammering. He did make her feel, make her feel she was real, make her know that she wanted more than she had.

And North wanted her, too.

Which was why she'd run from him.

Yet what she felt for him was profoundly different than anything she'd ever felt for another man. Suddenly she realized that she'd thought about him for months and months even when she hadn't admitted it to herself.

When her mother had sent her applications for an internship in Paris, Melody hadn't bothered to fill the papers out. Paris had suddenly seemed too far away. Why had she turned down so many wonderful opportunities?

She told North she wanted adventures with other less

controlling men, men who didn't press her to give what she couldn't give. The truth was she had zero interest in other men. Zero interest in being so far away.

Still, North was all wrong for her. Maybe he was only twenty-nine, maybe he was only seven years older than she was; still, because he'd assumed massive responsibilities at such a young age, he seemed a lifetime ahead of her. He'd managed a difficult family, employees, land, animals and lots of money. As a result, he seemed so sure of himself, he made her feel even younger and less certain than she did with other people.

He'd had no choice about choosing his career. She was trying to discover who she was and what she wanted to do with the rest of her life. Not that she really wanted to grow up. Childhood had seemed such a simple time. She'd been popular and loved until…

Until that long-ago afternoon when she'd been a sixth-grader, when a group of boys had followed her home from school. Their singsong taunts had set her heart to pounding like a drum. She'd run, but they'd been faster. It hadn't been long before one of them had tripped her, toppling her onto a shell driveway under the purple shade of a china-berry tree. Like a pack, they'd jumped her, their hands tugging at her skirt.

Her fingers clawed the gauzy curtains, and she forced her attention to her daddy, who was swinging his can of lighter fluid with a great flourish over the grate.

Mother would flip if she saw him do that.

Then Daddy struck a match, and flames whooshed four feet high. He jumped back. So did Melody.

On a deep shuddering breath, she opened her patio door and ran outside just as her mother tore out of the kitchen and began to shout about her precious rib eyes. North dashed out of the pool house and went straight to her father.

As North worked to get the fire back under control, Melody stood beneath the lush red bougainvillea that dripped from the balcony and watched the ripple of muscles in his broad brown shoulders and strong, wide chest. Long hours of brutal work in the sun had him leaner and tougher than ever.

Her mouth curved with amusement when she saw the thick gathers of the overlarge bathing suit he must've borrowed from Daddy bunching at his narrow waist.

Mother had a thing about staying slim. Maybe she had a point about putting Daddy on a diet.

When the fire was tamer, North stared across the yard at her, too. A different kind of panic lit his eyes when he saw her hiding from him amidst the purple-red blossoms in her mother's tight scarlet swimsuit with way too much of her bare bottom showing.

His beautiful mouth twisted.

She froze in that breathless instant before he tore his deep, dark gaze away and began poking at the fire again.

She jumped back inside. To find her mother's sarong, she told herself. After all, she needed a cover-up.

The next hour was filled with more little awkward moments when she joined North at the pool. When she removed the sarong, his black eyebrows slammed together. Then he dived into the pool.

Her parents were bickering good-humoredly beside the grill, but she was barely aware of them. A pang of regret tugged at her heart as she sank down on a chaise longue near a bed of ferns on the far side of the terrace.

North began swimming laps. Usually he worked so hard all day and was too tired for such vigorous exercise. She wondered if the only reason he was swimming like that was to avoid her.

He probably wanted to get through tonight and be done with her.

The same as she did.

Not so long ago, he would've knelt beside her and teased her. He would've wanted her attention, her smiles. Not so long ago, he'd loved her fiercely.

What made love like that stop? Had he simply willed it to stop?

Glumly she pasted on a smile and forced her gaze to slide past the translucent ferns toward her parents. Her father was tossing bits of rib eye down to Baby, the family's pedigreed Himalayan.

"Why does she meow if she doesn't want it?" Sam threw another chunk of meat down. "See—she's just sniffing and pawing at it."

"You have to cut Baby's steak into itsy-bitsy pieces," Dee Dee said, stealing his knife.

"What kind of sissy, no-good, snaggle-toothed cat—"

Baby had one crooked tooth that curled upward toward her nose like a miniature fang, making her look both darling and ridiculous.

"If you're mad at me," Dee Dee said, "don't attack my precious Baby. Give me that knife—"

"Ha! Don't think I'm going to use that knife after you use it on that cat's meat."

Geography. Suddenly it felt good to be home, good to have North here even if he didn't love her, Melody thought. The heavy air was warm and wet, pleasantly tropical. Wind rustled though the thick ferns and trees. Wind chimes tinkled. Her parents' jibes blended into the sounds of traffic from Ocean Drive, the scenic boulevard a block away that curved around the bay.

Almost she was a little girl again, safe and sound—here. Or a young woman in love for the first time. She remembered other suppers cooked outside, hamburgers made marvelous because North had been there. After dinner sometimes they'd put on music and had danced out by the pool. Sometimes he'd taken her for a spin in his pickup along the bay. Often they'd stopped at a seaside park and run, hand in hand, down to the beach as a full bright moon lit a golden path across black waves. Sometimes he'd stayed so late, he'd fallen asleep on the couch in the day and been there the next day when Sam got up.

Never looking her way, North swam furiously.

Turning her back to him, Melody revealed way too much hip and thigh.

Did she only imagine that North lowered his black head and swam even faster? The sun was low, but she rubbed lotion onto her legs anyway.

When he still wouldn't look, she got up and grabbed her mother's yellow air mattress and dragged it to the shallow end. Lying down on it carefully, she kicked herself toward the middle of the pool, straight into North's path.

Without looking up, he veered and swam even faster. She closed her eyes and just drifted, pretending she was enjoying the evening sounds and the way the water sloshed against her skin every time North swam by.

In reality she was remembering that terrible time when he'd dated her sister, Claire—the perfect, gorgeous Claire. Melody had pretended she hadn't cared about that, too. But all the time she'd felt so betrayed that he'd turned to Claire so soon after she'd jilted him. If he'd really loved her—

"Tell North it's nearly time for supper," her mother called.

Melody did a flutter kick and paddled with her hands until she got herself right in front of his path. As she waited for North there, her heart began to race absurdly.

He would have veered away from her again, only she thunked a knuckle on his wet black head. Instantly his big body slid to halt, his head stopping within inches of her parted legs.

"Supper," she said a little shyly.

"What's left of it," Dee Dee shouted at them. "Your father burned the rib eyes—as usual."

A heavy silence descended over the foursome. Sam, who was extremely sensitive about his cooking skills, wore a wounded frown as he flung the blackened steaks from the grill onto Dee Dee's platter. Abruptly North stood up and stomped toward the concrete stairs, dripping water. Melody raced after him and handed him her towel.

"Don't tell me how to cook, woman!" Sam thundered.

"Oh, dear," Melody whispered shyly to North.

North smiled. "I was wondering when he'd blow. A guy like your dad can only swallow so much."

"If you'd let me cook inside," Dee Dee countered.

"I'm retired, so I have time to barbecue."

"Who asked you to retire? I like to cook."

"Dee—"

Dee Dee raced toward the house in a huff. Sam grabbed the platter of steaks and followed her. "She's nicer to that damned cat than she ever is to me!"

"Alone at last," Melody said. "Just what you've been so scared of."

"I'm not scared."

"You look about as happy as Daddy did before he blew."

"That bad, huh?"

"Now that we're alone—you just might have to talk to me. A smile would be nice, too."

In spite of himself, North actually grinned at her.

"Ignoring you is as hard as talking to you."

"I wonder why?"

"I don't even want to know."

"Maybe because we loved each other for years and years," she whispered.

"You jilted me!"

"You turned to Claire fast enough!"

"So—how is the new bride?" he asked.

"Madly in love. Pregnant. Living in New Orleans."

They fell silent.

"We certainly made a mess of things," he said.

"I usually do...even when I try not to. You know that, North. You're so much older and more competent, you show me up...more than a less experienced kind of guy would."

As always when she even mentioned other guys, he scowled. When he lapsed into one of his moody silences, she could tell she was going to have to help him. Sometimes he couldn't get two words out of his mouth.

"What have you been doing...since—" she asked.

"Since *that* night?"

"I really want to know."

"Same as always. Just working."

"You're so brown," she said, her gaze drifting over his body.

"I'm outside a lot. You know that."

"And the big muscles?"

"From mucking stalls. Bailing hay. Fixing trucks. Working cows. Repairing fences."

"Don't you have cowboys?"

"I am a cowboy."

"Mr. Macho—always out to prove—"

"You don't know anything."

"Or maybe I do."

"Sometimes it's harder crunching numbers...thinking...than doing the actual work itself. Then there's this little camel...really he's a llama. He's a newborn and having a tough time. I get up every morning to feed him. He's not putting on weight."

"Why not?"

"He needs his mama's milk straight out of his mama, I guess."

"I can see you're worried about him."

"He was real shy at first. He's getting used to me." He looked at her. "He climbed into my lap once.... It's ridiculous."

"No, being tenderhearted is never ridiculous," she said softly. "I'd like to meet your llama."

"Little Camel."

"Little Camel," she repeated.

"What about you?"

"After India...Manhattan...Boston...then home to Austin.... The big cities weren't as exciting as I thought they'd be, so I didn't stay long. So, mostly, it's just been the same old stuff for me, too.''

"The same park job?"

"I just quit. Two weeks ago."

"For good, I hope. I never liked you working…"

When she frowned, he stopped.

"You didn't like that one park because of its clothing optional beach."

"Men go there. They take off their clothes."

"I worked the ticket booth. Besides, it wasn't like I worked there every day."

"Why didn't it bother you that those guys strutted around with nothing when you wouldn't let me…"

"Maybe if you'd been content just to strut." She giggled. "Maybe you should be glad I was trying to get over my…er…hang-up and get used to the idea of naked men and…"

"Usually a virgin gets comfortable about that with the man she loves."

"There aren't rules for life—Bertie."

"You taught me that. That's for damn sure. You wear the sexiest underwear in the universe…and can't stand sex."

"Other people's rules don't work for me."

"So, you're making up a set of your own as you go?"

As he stared at her, she lowered her gaze to the ripple of hard teak flesh that laced his chest and shoulders. All of a sudden she imagined that sleek, bronzed body on one of those limestone shelves at the park's clothing optional beach. How glorious he'd be out there—naked.

Why didn't he put his shirt on? Why did he have to be so virile and dark, so honed with muscle—so male.

She flushed, and that made her angry. "Maybe I can't work my problems out—the usual way."

"Keep staring, darlin'." He grinned. "Dirty thoughts?"

"Of course not."

"Hope springs eternal."

"All you ever think about is sex."

When his white grin broadened, she felt wild for him. Which made her even more uncomfortable. She knew that if he'd touched her or tried to kiss her, she would have died from the thrill of it even though it would have scared her.

She hadn't dated since him. All of a sudden she knew why. She wanted him even though she was scared of sex. She licked her lips and then rubbed her brow.

"It's okay...what you did," he said, "your wanting to break up. It was for the best. I see that now. Like I told you, I need a woman."

She frowned.

"We're too different," he persisted. "What we want is too different."

"Really?" She swallowed hard.

"I wanted you in bed."

"And now you don't?" She flushed, feeling strange and hurt, which was ridiculous.

"Now I just want you to be happy," he murmured.

For a second she felt so shy and awkward, she couldn't think of anything else to say, so she said the first thing that popped into her mind. Which was stupid.

"I'm sorry I ruined your relaxing evening with my parents."

"I guess we'd better go in and get to relaxing. I'll get dressed."

"You look good."

"Dirty thoughts again?" The warmth in his teasing voice was sweet and familiar.

"I do have dirty thoughts," she admitted. "Oh, Bertie, I'm all mixed up."

"I won't argue that point." But he smiled down at her with genuine affection.

"We used to be such good friends," she said. "I've missed that."

"Me, too." He tensed. "But we can't be friends. Not when I still feel—"

"You do?"

A quick heat washed and ebbed in her cheeks.

Before he could answer, Dee Dee opened the door and called out to them, "Y'all coming?"

"What do you feel?"

"It doesn't matter." His voice was colder. "It can't matter."

He was right, of course. So why did she feel curiously deflated?

"I'm hungry. That's all," he said. "Starved." His eyes lingered on her. "Let's go eat. At least that's something we can still do together without getting into trouble."

"Maybe I want to get into trouble."

"You always say that. You always back down."

"What if I didn't?"

"It's too late. I've got a new girl—Maria. Everybody says she's perfect for me."

Her heart slammed painfully. Her stomach knotted. "Oh, North, I—I'm so happy for you."

Four

North felt so tired. The den was icy cold, refreshingly so after the long hot day. The Woodses' couch was way too comfortable all of a sudden. North was glad dinner was over and the Woodses and their impossible sexy daughter were all out of the dining room. Even sprawled out on their extra-long sofa, his legs felt cramped from sitting still so long underneath that antique table.

Voices were talking in North's head, but he was too drowsy to be turned-on by *her* to heed them.

Say goodbye and leave.

In a minute.

You shouldn't have trailed so dutifully after Melody down that flowery hall when Dee Dee and Sam came in here.

If you don't git, you'll be trapped for sure, pardner.

Obstinately he pillowed his hands behind his black head and tried to ignore Melody so he could make sense out of the Woodses' conversation that was getting more rambling and less coherent with every drink.

Melody had gotten really quiet when he'd told her about Maria. All through the interminable dinner she'd just sat still and alert, barely picking at her spinach salad, not daring even to look at him. Maybe because he and Melody had been so strained, Dee Dee and Sam had drunk too much and taken over.

Say goodbye. Maria's perfect for you.

Dee Dee's voice was shrill; Sam's speech was slurred but was going strong.

Smile. It's the second best thing you can do with your lips.

All of a sudden, North couldn't take his eyes off Melody. In the shadowy light, she seemed so young and vulnerable and yet utterly delectable. So lost and needy.

Like him.

So kissable.

His physical reaction to her bothered him. Maybe he was too bone-weary to fight it. He'd worked too hard and long in the sun. He'd swum too vigorously and eaten too much as well. Suddenly he felt incredibly at home on the Woodses' couch.

At least he knew where Melody was for a change.

Not that he cared. Maria was going to be his girl. As he'd said, she was perfect.

When Dee Dee and Sam suddenly stopped talking, North felt he had to say something to get them going again, so he could stay.

"So, how do you like retirement, Sam?"

They both bristled, feathers straight up, like two cocks in a ring.

North was soon so sleepy he caught only fragments of their tense answers.

"—great...great—"

"—I wish Sam still had some hobbies—"

"—you have enough for both of us, spending money—"

"—bet you're working hard, too hard, on that big ranch—"

''—from before sunup to after sundown, sir. Day after day—''

''—those long hot days finally catching up to you—''

Their voices blurred. All he saw was Melody, sitting stiffly at the other end of the couch in that sexy red one-piece suit that fit her pert breasts like a glove and left too much of her legs exposed. More than anything he wanted to hold her.

If he fell asleep, he could stay.

The Woodses' voices softened, and North's chest began to feel very heavy. Then it began to rise and fall more rhythmically. Vaguely he was aware of Dee Dee and Sam whispering and then tiptoeing silently past him. Of Melody staying.

He wanted to pull her closer, to feel the heat of her body next to his as they lay there together. But when he finally murmured her name, she was gone, and there was only the hum of the deliciously cold air conditioner.

The den got colder and darker. When he opened his eyes a long while later, Melody was back, kneeling beside him, looking more gorgeous than ever in a red knit blouse with spaghetti straps, white short skirt edged with red rickrack, and strappy red sandals. Her reddish gold hair was piled high, caught in a scarlet ribbon, loose tendrils of the silky stuff spilling over her shoulders. Was she wearing black lace underneath?

''Why red tonight? You hate red,'' he muttered thickly running a fingertip beneath her chin even as he wondered about her underwear.

She shivered.

''Yes.''

''How come?''

Her smoky-blue eyes darkened.

When he kept stroking her, she swallowed. ''The suit was Mother's.'' She swallowed. ''The blouse is hers, too. I haven't unpacked yet.''

''And you'll probably let a year go by before you do,''

he teased, remembering how she had a bad habit of putting things off. "Is it morning? How long did I sleep, darlin'?"

"A couple of hours."

"What?" He jumped up. Sitting forward, he raked his hands through his hair.

"You must be awful tired, North."

"Long days," he admitted. "Long nights, too." Long lonely nights. Then there were those strange, surreal, wild nights chasing the Midnight Bandit.

"Maria?"

"Work."

"So, you're neglecting your perfect girlfriend, too?"

"We just started dating." Why the hell had he admitted that?

"Hey, I don't want to talk about her."

Struck anew by Melody's beauty, he reached out and touched her lips with his fingertip. She looked like an angel with that halo of hair glowing around her face.

Smile. It's the second best thing you can do with your lips.

He jerked his hand from that luscious, swollen mouth.

"I came to see if you're all right," she said gently. "To tell you goodbye. I'm going out."

He stole a peek at his watch under his white cuff. It was past midnight. "At this hour? Alone?"

"Not alone."

That made him fiercer.

"You could come with us." She hesitated as if her invitation had been accidental, impulsive. "I mean...only if you wanted to."

"*Us?* Where? Who?"

"Us. Cathy and me. Out dancing."

Damn. "Just Cathy?" He didn't much like Cathy Murano. He didn't consider her a good influence. She had sex on the brain and considered herself a fount of wisdom in that department. But she and Melody had been friends since preschool, and Melody had a soft spot for old friends.

At least they didn't have dates. Not that he cared.

Then it hit him. Maybe they were going out to look for guys.

"You're going to a bar, aren't you?" he asked.

Melody shrugged, causing a thin red strap to fall off her shoulder. "You know Cathy."

"And you know what I think of her, too."

"Don't start. You're not my boyfriend anymore. You've got Maria."

Smile. It's the second... He blocked that refrain.

"Right." Why was that always so hard to remember when Melody was anywhere near?

A minute ago he'd been dead tired. He'd given her the impression he intended to get serious about Maria, who really was perfect for him if only... The last thing he needed was to go dancing with Melody at some pickup place.

"Yes," he growled.

"Yes?"

"Yes, I'll go."

"Oh, dear."

"What?"

When she burst out laughing, she looked so beautiful he forgot to wonder why he'd worried that she'd seemed so alarmed at first.

He found out soon enough once they parked in front of a squatty, windowless, black building downtown and saw the huge hot pink letters throbbing as if they'd come to life. The Liquid Poodle's marquee was advertising a drag show at 1:00 a.m.

"A drag show? Tell me we aren't going to a gay bar," he muttered.

"We aren't going to a gay bar," Melody teased.

"We sure as hell are," he growled.

"So—you told me to lie."

He got out and went around the car and opened her door. "How come you two chose a gay bar?"

"Guys in gay bars don't hit on girls."

"Oh, wise up, Mel," Cathy said from the back seat, smacking her chewing gum as she pushed her own door open. She paused to blow a big pink bubble which Melody popped with a white polished fingernail. "Sometimes they do."

North lifted an eyebrow.

On that cheery note, Cathy, who was tall and dark with spiky, red-tipped black hair and a tiny silver ring through her left eyebrow, slid out of the car. While North locked the car, Cathy breezed ahead of them to try to talk the bouncer into lowering her cover charge.

"You go to these places with her often?" North asked.

"She called me. We both felt like dancing tonight."

"I forgot—you're the extrovert."

"You're getting nicer. Usually you call me the exhibitionist, the show-off."

"You're that, too."

"Maybe someday, I'll put on a private show just for you."

"Been there. Done that. Please just swear you won't do it in public again."

"I swear."

"Why don't I feel the least bit reassured?"

"'Cause you're a worrywart, Rancher Black! Cheer up. I mean that in a good way."

"What if somebody sees me here?" he said.

"You're with me. So, you're safe."

"You have a funny definition of safe."

Inside the bar, the beat of the music was all powerful. North liked rock, but this industrial hip-hop had no melody and was blasting so loud he had to jam bits of paper napkin into his ears. Not that the lyrics were worth listening to anyway.

Other than the loud music, the bar seemed dead.

"Not many people tonight," he said to Melody as he eyed the empty tables and the men sitting alone at the bar.

"We're here," she said brightly.

North cast a suspicious eye on the other patrons, who were mostly men. Guys with earrings. Guys in sleeveless T-shirts that showed off sculpted brown arms and a few creative tattoos. Guys with lean waists and hips in low-slung, flared jeans prowled the edges of the room. They were watching him, too.

Dark lights made everybody's earrings and white shirts glow, including his. The weird effect made him feel exposed.

He was glad he didn't see anybody he knew.

"Now don't panic, Bertie."

"Who the hell's panicking?" He rubbed his collar.

She put a fingertip on his brown nose. "I know that look."

"You ought to. You can get kinda panicky yourself."

They stared at each other's lips, and he wondered if she was remembering lying in his bed, snuggled close, his hands all over her. He took her arm and led her upstairs, so he could keep an eye on the action. Cathy followed them.

The men sat on their stools drinking and smoking, not talking. Nobody danced.

Then a waiter with stark white hair and intense light eyes swaggered up to their table. "What'll you have?"

North quickly ordered three beers. "Straight out of the bottle. No glasses."

The man's laser blue-white eyes burned into North's. The boy grinned. "Gotcha."

Cathy excused herself to go to the ladies' room.

"Brave lady," North murmured in an undertone as he glared at the sign above the men's room.

Melody threaded her fingers around his. "Let's dance."

The empty dance floor was ringed by silent men, their shirts eerily aglow.

"You've got to be out of your mind."

"Then I'll dance by myself."

"Don't you dare—"

"Bertie-boy, your earplugs are glowing."

"Bertie was bad enough, little darlin'...."

"Bertie's cute," she breathed. "So are you." Her eyes glinted with mischief as she rested her hand lightly on his forearm.

He forgot where they were. He forgot everything but her. His heart pulsed from her light touch. Overhead spots started to flash.

Before he could grab her wrist and hold on to her, the brat was gone. Almost instantly, the impertinent exhibitionist was in the middle of the dance floor. When somebody aimed a spotlight on her, she winked at North.

When he scowled down at her, she closed her eyes, extended both hands toward him and began undulating to the wild jungle beat.

All by herself.

In front of all those guys.

North's blood ran cold as he stared at her. It turned to ice when he realized the guys weren't watching her.

They were watching him.

The black walls seemed to close in on him as everybody's white shirts seemed to brighten with an otherworldly brilliance. Nose rings and earrings flamed blue.

When a blond fellow in a radiant tank top with light eyes and an eyebrow ring smiled and then swaggered toward him, North shoved back his stool and raced toward Melody.

Three long strides had North in the middle of that dance floor with Melody who beamed at him playfully.

"It was only the waiter," she giggled.

He grabbed her by the waist and pulled her to him.

Big mistake—even here, even with guys gawking at him, he was instantly more aware of Melody than of anything else in the room. Through his jeans, he felt the heat of her pelvis, the heat of her legs.

She put her mouth against his ear. "What about your new, perfect girl?"

"Who?"

"Maria."

"Oh—her. Forget I ever mentioned her." He pulled her close.

For an instant Melody's smoky-blue eyes darkened as she caught the rhythm and swayed into him. Hips molded to his, their bodies writhing in perfect harmony, she felt better and better to him. The throbbing beat played havoc with his other senses.

He'd wanted a woman. She'd been a shy girl.

Something told him the rules of the game they'd always played together were about to change.

Too late. She'd done him wrong.

Then he felt her lips against his collar. Her body was sleek and warm. His body didn't care what she'd done.

Smile. It's the second best thing you can do with your lips.

The jukebox changed. Somebody played their song, and he forgot where they were and what she'd done. He closed his eyes and forgot everything but Melody.

Dancing, the music, the woman, his own longing stripped him of the last of his logical sense. He responded against his will.

"Oh, Bertie. Bertie...Bertie...Bertie..."

Her hands caressed his neck. Her breath was warm against his throat.

Here we go again.

She was putting on one of her performances. Getting him all worked up—for nothing. He was twenty-nine. He knew better. He wanted more.

He'd loved her. For as long as he could remember, he'd loved her. But his love hadn't been enough. She hadn't wanted him enough. She'd wanted adventures, an exciting life, not some rancher tied to his land, his family, to his duty. And not sex.

His brain screamed at him to take her home, but his flesh

was weak. She tantalized him with her sweet promises. And as always, he was a sucker for lost causes.

So, he swirled her into a dark corner where they danced alone, where he got hotter and hotter whether the songs were slow or fast. Only vaguely was he aware of Cathy coming up to them and whispering through the shadows that she was going to another bar with a friend.

"Why don't we go somewhere, too, Bertie?" Melody whispered.

"Where?"

"Wherever you want."

"All right." His voice was soft even though his body throbbed to have her.

He grabbed her by the hand and led her outside. The warm, salt-laden breeze felt heavy and yet fresh after the smoky bar. Glad to be outside, he inhaled deeply. So did she.

He wanted to kiss her so badly he hurt, to push for more as he always had in the past.

Instead he walked her to her car in silence. After he helped her inside, he got behind the wheel. When he drove her to her parents' home, she seemed surprised.

"But I thought you wanted—"

"Not anymore," he lied even as he felt he was dying inside because he wanted her so much.

"Because of your new, perfect girl—"

"Don't bring anybody else into this."

"I didn't. You did."

"Be fair." He brushed his hand against her velvet soft cheek for the last time and felt its dampness wetting his finger. Tears. God, she was killing him.

"Good night, Melody," he rasped. "Have a nice life."

"You, too." Her glassy blue eyes caught the night light and reflected pain as intense with torment as his own. "And y-you take good care of that baby llama, you hear," she murmured.

"I will. I swear it."

"Goodbye then..." The sheen of tears glazing her eyes cut through him like a knife.

"Mel, don't cry—"

"Don't go to Maria. Not...not tonight."

"What?"

"I had fun tonight...with you," she said. "Like always."

He nodded and swallowed the hard lump in his throat. He didn't speak as she opened her door and got out and ran up the walk.

At the door she turned as if willing him to weaken and change his mind.

Clenching the steering wheel, he waited until the foyer lights were snuffed out before he opened the car door. Only then did he get out and walk ever so slowly toward his own truck.

It was over.

At last.

Five

"**Y**ou don't understand, Cathy. I'm not like you. I'm still a…a…" Melody's heart pounded as she lay on her bed, pressing the receiver against her ear as she toyed with the cord, which wound between her legs. "Well," she whispered. "You know, the V-word."

The wind had picked up. Outside the palm fronds clattered. Her parents' two-story, wooden house was talking to her, too. Melody held her breath as she waited, but Cathy was silent.

"Say something!"

"I knew you were hung-up, Mel. But…but…this is too much! This is the twenty-first century! You can't still be a—!"

Melody put her hand over the mouthpiece. "Shh! What if my dad picks up the phone?"

"What about North? I thought you went to his place *that* night—"

"But I didn't sleep with him," she whispered.

"But you let me think— He broke up with Claire for you."

"It's why we broke up in the first place. Why we never really got back together after Claire."

Cathy snickered. "You're twenty-two. You've got to be joking!"

Melody closed her eyes. "Don't laugh at me...please."

Cathy smacked her gum. "I'm not. This is serious. This is not normal. You know that, don't you? Have you considered therapy?"

Melody swallowed. "You sound like Mother! I can't talk about this to some stranger! It's hard enough telling you!"

"You've gotta do something about this, babe. Right away."

"Like what?"

"Like face the fact North wants you. Real bad. The way he was dancing... The way he couldn't take his eyes off you, not for a second... God, you two got *me* hot. Just watching you— He's on testosterone overload. He's hurting, babe."

"He drove me straight home."

"So? You two have a history."

"He dated my sister. My perfect sister."

"Because you jilted him."

"Because... Oh, I don't know what's wrong with me. He and I don't communicate."

"That's the best reason I know to have sex! You've gotta go for it."

"Believe me, I've tried."

"So—don't quit. I've got a feeling you're on a roll tonight."

"But—"

"Just go over there."

"To North's? What would I say to him? Do?"

"Just go! Then play it by ear. Put on some music. Guys like..."

"They like what?"

"Sexual favors. You know. Show him how much you care."

"I don't know how. I always get scared when he tries something."

"So you try something! It's not like you need lessons. You were born knowing how. Besides, North knows how."

"But I don't know anything but stuff other girls talk about or stuff I see in movies. And when it happens it always makes me feel sick. This is easy for you. It's hard for me. I—I don't know why."

"You think too much." Cathy paused. "It gets easier. You've just gotta practice. You'll like it."

"I—I don't know where to start."

"From first base. Kiss him. Go now."

"I can't."

More gum smacking and bubble blowing. "You mentioned movies. And that got me thinking about those videos you stole out of your parents' closet when you were sifting through their stuff."

"That was years ago!"

"Not all that long really. We watched that one about that girl named Ala over and over two months ago!"

"I didn't! You did!"

"You watched it through your fingers!"

"It was so disgusting. What they did. What she did."

"Guys don't think so. Go now!"

"I don't think—"

"Do you want that Maria, whoever she is, to get him?"

"Maria?" Did the whole world know about Maria?

A gum bubble popped. "Jeff's telling everybody about Miss Perfection—especially your friends."

"He's never liked me."

"Well, he likes Maria, and she's gorgeous. He says she's been after North since forever. She's got a great big ranch right next to his, and it's almost as big as El Dorado. Besides being impressed with her land, Jeff says she's real sexy. Big at the top. If you don't do something to knock

North's socks off and fast, she's gonna get him, babe! A
smart woman knows how to hook a lonely man with sex
and then reel him in real slow.''

"But I can't!"

"I'll tell you what to do. If other people can do it, you
can, too. Drink a glass of wine. Watch the video. Let it
spark some creativity. Then imagine yourself and North
doing—"

"Cathy, you really are disgusting."

"Maybe so, but I'm not frigid. My guys like me."

Melody gasped. "Guys? The only man I've ever really
wanted is—"

"Go over there. Put on some music. Start dancing. It'll
happen. You can't stay eleven years old forever."

"Eleven years old—" Melody's voice trailed off. "Why
did you pick that age?"

"I gotta go," Cathy said. "Just remember sex is the
hook that is the main weapon in a fishergirl's box of lures.
Use it or lose him. And you don't have to tell him you're
still a...a...the V-word."

Cathy hung up.

Eleven.

Melody had been eleven that day she'd worn those red
cotton panties to school and Randy Hunter had glimpsed
bright ruffles under her skirt when she'd been jumping
rope. He'd told some other guys, and they'd all wanted to
see her panties, too.

So, they'd followed her home and scared her so bad she
still couldn't—

Maybe if she had just one glass of wine...

A little dazed, Melody lay still on the den couch, her
hands covering her eyes, staring into blackness, instead of
at those awful images flickering on the television screen.

Why was sex such a big deal?

A low moan broke the silence when she finally managed

to part her fingers and stare through them at the wiggling couple.

Tongues. Hands. Lips.

She couldn't watch the odious pair.

Forcing her fingers wider, she stared at a seedy-looking black-haired man unzipping his jeans while a brassy red-head unbuttoned her blouse. Their eyes were dead, their complexions waxen. But they tongued their lips, straining to give the illusion of sexual ecstasy to their viewers.

Melody tensed. She shut her eyes.

They were faking it. She couldn't watch them smile when their hearts weren't in it. Oh, they knew what to do, what part to put where. But it was all so mechanical, so contrived and spiritless. Where was love, tenderness?

What did love and tenderness have to do with sex?

Cathy had said to imagine other people she knew doing this. Melody tightened her fingers over her eyes and re-sisted that advice.

Instead of the woman on her television screen, Melody saw a little girl running down a tree-lined street as fast as she could. She heard cruel, jeering voices behind her. Four bigger boys wearing mirrored sunglasses. She felt hunted, terrified. Then they were on top of her.

North had come, and the boys had run. They hadn't re-ally done anything but look at her red panties and laugh. Just the same, she'd felt violated. She hadn't been sure exactly what they'd even intended. But that hadn't stopped her from filling in all the empty blanks in her imagination with terror and shame.

She'd pushed her skirt down and gotten herself more or less together before North had seen her. He'd wanted to know why they'd chased her and what they'd done to her. She hadn't told him. After all, it was her fault for wearing the pretty new red panties to school. Her behavior had been even every bit as shameful as theirs.

"Your heart's racing like a rabbit's," North had whis-pered as he helped her up.

"I'm fine."

"Did they hurt you?"

She'd shaken her head.

"These yours?" In his hand he'd held a pair of mirrored sunglasses.

She'd screamed and thrown herself into his arms and sobbed. Then she'd pushed him away. "Don't tell Mother."

"But—"

"You know how she is. She'll come up to the school. Then everybody'll know—"

"Know what?"

About my red panties.

She'd taken the sunglasses and thrown them down. Then she'd stomped on them until nothing was left but glittering bits. "I just don't want people to know. That's all."

When Melody opened her eyes, the man on the television was pushing the woman down, nestling her face against his waist. When she licked her lips, he forced her to—

She shut her eyes. When she peered through her fingers again, he no longer looked like he was having to fake ecstasy.

In a single fluid movement Melody got up and yanked the obscene tape from the tape player. She set it down slowly and buried her face in her hands again.

The wind continued drumming through the palms. The house creaked. But more than that she felt the mad thumping of her own heart.

North was in town tonight, in his apartment. He'd be gone in a day or two.

She knew she should get undressed for bed, but if she did, she wouldn't be able to sleep. She would think of North, of the way he'd looked at her so hungrily when she'd answered the front door, of the way he'd shoved her against the wall, of the way he hadn't looked at her when she'd lain beside the pool and he'd swum.

Confusing images bombarded her.

North hurtling his huge body at her on the dance floor; North holding her close.

North in her car, his big brown hand gentle on her cheek, his look of profound pain when he'd seen her tears.

She imagined him alone now, lying in his bed fast asleep.

Was he dreaming of Maria? Dreaming of Maria doing all those things that man in the video had had the cheap-looking actress do?

Picking up the bottle of wine, Melody carried it to her bedroom. There she poured herself another glass. Then she opened the drawer that contained all North's old pictures. She had ones from every stage of his life.

When he'd been six, his ears had stuck out through his thick black hair. He'd told her he'd been a brat back then. When he'd been ten, his daddy's big cowboy hat had swallowed him. When he'd been twelve, a darkly slim boy with a solemn face stood stiffly holding on to his daddy's big deer rifle.

In all his older pictures his expression was grave. It was as if he'd lost some vital spark. His college pictures were of a stern young man. Melody reshuffled. She preferred his laughing baby pictures. What would it take to make the real man look as happy as the little boy in the pictures?

The most recent photograph was one Claire had taken of him standing by his pickup, holding a rifle in one hand and a dead wild turkey in the other.

Melody didn't like hunting or his grim expression, but he looked so broad-shouldered and lean in that picture, she'd kept it anyway. Clasping it against her breasts, she opened her patio door and stepped outside into the wild, humid night.

For a long time she stood there, her hair billowing. Frowning, she thought about what that couple had done on the video.

Sexual favors. You know. Show him how much you care.

She bit her bottom lip. Then she poured herself another glass of wine.

What if she called a cab and showed up at his apartment? What if she took the key out from under his flowerpot and let herself inside? What if she slid into bed and made wild passionate love to him?

You tried that once before. You failed miserably.

But the wine sent dizzying sensations all through her. She went back inside and turned on her radio. The thudding beat of the same song she and North had danced to in the bar filled the room. She felt warm and crazy and feminine and needy and wild. She threw herself onto her bed and grabbed her favorite teddy bear and tried to fight the demon in her brain that told her to go to him.

The minutes dragged by. She thought of the stark longing in his eyes when he'd said goodbye. Still, he was stubborn, and he'd made his mind up about her. If only she could stop thinking about him, stop feeling—

Why did she feel so jittery and restless? An hour later and she was up pacing.

If she didn't do something—

What if he threw her out?

What if he didn't?

One minute North was sound asleep and dreaming of Melody. Not the innocent, shy exhibitionist, but a real woman with sultry eyes who knew what to do as she writhed underneath him.

The next minute he heard his front door click open and shut. When he heard the jingle of his truck keys, he knew the intruder must've stepped on them, for it was his habit to leave them on the floor by the front door.

Next he heard the soft whispers of footsteps approaching his bedroom. Springing out of bed, he went for his holstered Colt in his top drawer.

Only it wasn't there. He must have forgotten it and left it in his glove compartment.

Quickly he crossed his bedroom to wait in the dark corner by the door.

The wind was beating against his windowpanes as the ghostly figure stepped inside and glided toward his bed. He heard a faint indrawn breath and then a little gasp right before he lunged.

Even before he knocked her down, he knew the intruder was a woman. Still, he pushed her onto the bed, rolled her over, grabbed her wrists and pinned her there. When she tried to scream, his hand covered her mouth.

"Who the hell—"

"It's me, you big idiot—Melody."

Her face was pale, her hair tousled, her eyes as dark and defiant and sultry as his dream girl's. She still wore that sexy white skirt with the red rickrack that had gotten him so wired.

"What do you want?"

"You."

His jaw knotted. "Whoa!" He let her go.

She sprang free of him, got up and backed quickly toward the window.

"You sure scared me," she said a little shakily.

"Likewise. How the hell did you get in?"

"Ah, Bertie, I know all your secrets—"

His heart began to slam, his body to harden. "I hardly think so," he muttered.

She ran a hand down her throat and fiddled with the low neckline of her red blouse. Her hair was iridescent in the dim glow of the moon. He watched the play of her white fingertips and the flicker of fire those glistening moons made against her breasts.

She seemed to be recovering more quickly than he.

"Well, I know where your secret key is...that flower-pot... I know that your ivy died."

"Because I wasn't here to water it. So—"

She floated soundlessly toward his balcony and leaned against his wall there. Moonlight washed her and made her skin glow like alabaster. Her breasts swelled against her knit top.

His throat went dry. "Melody, we said goodbye—"

"I wouldn't blame you if you sent me away." Her voice
was small, young, innocent and yet slow and sexy, too. Her
long-lashed, smoky dark eyes were erotic as hell.

"I wouldn't blame me, either," he growled. "Go home
before you get into more trouble than you can handle."

"You once told me that you wanted a woman," she
purred, her eyes smoldering with promises now. "Not a
girl."

The voice, those eyes, everything she did— All of a sudden, fool that he was, she had him panting hard. "More
than once—"

"Well, I—I'm here now...."

"It's too late," he muttered thickly. "Way too late."

"What if I want to be your woman?"

"Mel, we tried this before—"

"Again. And again. I know. Please, don't send me
away."

"Then make it easy for me. I don't want to hurt you.
Just go home."

"But I sent the cab away."

"I'll drive you."

Again her gaze locked with his. "I've got a better idea.
Let me prove I'm all grown-up."

She seemed so young and eager, so fragile. What if she
went to someone else in this mood? It would be so easy to
scare her forever.

"Come here," he whispered helplessly.

When she reached him, he took her in his arms and hungrily kissed her mouth, and reeled with shock and fiery
sensation.

She was like a lightning bolt. Liquid fire pulsed in his
blood. "You're so beautiful," he said, startled.

"Oh, North—"

"You are." She was warm; she tasted like the sweetest
wine. Desire flooded him as it always did when she teased
him like this.

When he tried to push free, a low moan escaped her lips. His hands tightened around her waist, and he rubbed her against him. She began to tremble and that got him shaking.

With an effort he stopped. "If I fall for this little seduction game, you'll chicken out—"

"Maybe I'll surprise you."

"It won't be the first time."

"Or the last."

Her lips parted. What if, for once, he let her take the lead? When he stood still, she kissed him.

She did indeed taste of wine.

"You've been drinking, darlin'. You never drink."

"Who says courage doesn't come in a bottle?"

"It's a bad habit—drinking."

"I'm a big girl. Maybe it's time...I acquired a few bad habits. Maybe it's time I found out what big girls do in their spare time."

His gut clenched. "Are you still a—?"

"The V-word?"

He nodded.

She licked her lips. "Sort of."

"What's that supposed to mean?"

"I've always figured that sex was overrated."

"So you've been experimenting."

"Maybe."

"You're lying. This whole thing is a ruse, a setup. Like before."

"There's only one way for you to be sure."

"All right." He fixed her with a hard-as-nails glare. Expecting her to run, he ripped off his pajama bottoms.

But she stepped closer. Taking them from him, she tossed them out of the way. Then while he watched her face, she put her hand on his waist and let it glide lower until her fingers circled him.

He froze.

She stared as if she'd shocked herself, too. He drew in a deep breath and reminded himself to do nothing.

Finally she began stroking him. Her caressing fingers were so skilled that when she squeezed him, he almost came.

"Don't you hurt me, little darlin'," he whispered.

"Had enough, Bertie boy?" Then she giggled and let him go and scampered over to his bed.

He watched the graceful movement of her arms as she pushed her blouse down and pulled her skirt up. When she lay down on his bed, she drew a leg up and began to hum the song they'd danced to in the bar.

"Do you want me to put on some music?" he whispered.

"Why don't you come over here so we can make our own?"

Two long strides had him beside her. "I don't believe this."

Languidly she stretched full length across his bed. "Believe it." She took his hand and pulled him down.

"Melody, why? Why tonight?"

Her eyes were hard and intent upon his face, but she couldn't seem to answer. Instead she rolled into his big tan body and threaded her fingertips into the bristly hair of his chest.

"I—I think I always thought you'd devour me, or that this would give you the upper hand."

He was dark and tough while she was slim and fragile. He'd felt old, grown-up, for nearly as long as he could remember. She was fresh, new—able to bring out a part of him he thought long dead. When she climbed on top of him and straddled him, a throbbing, burning excitement began to build inside him.

Then she closed her eyes and touched his face, his throat, her hands moving as lovingly as a blind woman until he went wild beneath her featherlight strokes. He clenched his teeth, determined not to show it. Somehow, aside from his heavier breathing, he was able to lie still while she made love to him.

When her burning lips followed the path of her hands, he stiffened, gasped, and then closed his eyes, too.

Slowly she eased lower. Always before they'd gotten this far, he'd been overcome by his own passion and had sought to control her and push for more.

Not tonight. Tonight he gritted his teeth, and knotted his fingers, mindless with desire and yet afraid of doing anything to frighten her.

Slowly, ever so slowly her golden head and wet tongue trailed the length of his abdomen. She kissed him wetly, sucking his nipples, kissing him everywhere until she sent tremors coursing through his body.

When she hesitated, he reached for her, his hands tangling in the silken waves of her hair. Her scent flooded his nostrils. His breath grew ragged. Still, he sensed she had to be in control.

He shot her a glance and read alarm in her overlarge eyes. He was gut sure she was about to bolt. But when he didn't try to force her, she gave another of those whispery little gasps and scooting farther down his legs, buried her face in his groin. When her mouth closed over him, he groaned.

Stunned, and yet thrilled beyond words, he sank deeper into the mattress and after a while, her lips began to move back and forth with sensuous expertise proving, that after all, she knew exactly what to do. And yet she wasn't simply going through the motions. Reverently, gently, she was making the most exquisite love to him. Sex like that wasn't possible unless—

Hunger surged through him. From tip to base, her tongue was gentle yet scalding hot. She'd hardly started, and he was about to explode.

"Darlin', let me kiss you, too." He put his hands on her shoulders.

When she shook her head, he nearly lost his mind. She'd been stubborn about not making love. She was just as stubborn now.

A wise voice in the back of his head told him to play it smart and lie back and enjoy it, that he'd waited a helluva long time for what this particular lady was offering, that if tonight was her turn to pleasure him, some night, there would be a night that was his turn to return the favor.

So, he changed position slightly and put his hands in her hair, moving her head to and fro, thrusting until he shuddered in completion.

She gasped. When she lifted her face, he stared at her in wonder. She brought a fingertip to her lips. Then, wrapping her in his arms, so that their bodies touched everywhere, he began to kiss her, to coax her. He'd never been sure of her before this moment.

Why? Why had she done this?

Suddenly, she stopped him and nestled her head against his chest as if to hide. He lay still and held her, stunned, wondering at the sheer loveliness of her, at the loveliness of what she'd done.

He stroked her hair. She was beautiful, and skillful at this, amazingly so. Once he had loved her with all his heart. He had wanted to marry her. He had always sensed how warm and sensitive and exquisite she'd be if he ever got her in bed.

Tonight she had sent him over some wild edge. She was really something. Once—and he was already an addict.

"Look at me, little darlin'." He lifted her chin, but she wouldn't look at him.

He grinned. "You want more. Same as I do."

She shook her head fervently.

Again he wondered why she had come to him? Done this? Tonight? When they'd both agreed it was over? After they'd said goodbye?

Why? Was it some new game?

Smile. It's the second best thing you can do with your lips.

Why had she said that at the door? Who had taught her to think like that?

As he lay in the dark, his happiness and hope gave way to disillusionment and doubt. What had she said earlier when he'd been so dazed by her beauty— That she was only *sort of* a virgin now, that she'd been experimenting.

Sort of? Who else had she done this with? What else had she done with him, with them? Was tonight like her job at the park? Another step in ridding herself of her hang-ups?

"Damn you," he whispered.

Her eyes widened.

He tore himself free of her. He had to know, no matter how unpleasant the truth was. Being a man, quite naturally, he stuck his size twelve foot in his mouth and asked her straight out.

"Why'd you come over here? Where the hell did you learn a trick like that? Were you pretending I was somebody else? Somebody more exciting? Who taught—"

Dark eyebrows arched in confusion and then indignation. "Who taught—"

"Well, you're too damn good to be a rank beginner."

"What?"

"I said you've got quite a knack for it, darlin'."

"Is that what you think?" Her sexy voice was low and choked. She continued to stare at him with those frightened, wide, glazed eyes, as if her emotions tore at her.

"You're too damn good," he repeated levelly. "I'm not the first man you tried this on, am I?"

She went even whiter, as if he'd struck her. Her eyes were wet as she scooted away.

"Well, what of it? You weren't! And I'm glad!" She notched her chin up. "I—I had a great teacher! Lots and lots of them! In Paris, India, Austin… All you did was lie there."

"All I did was lie there—"

Rage howled inside him. Hurt, too. His stomach tightened. As she scrambled even farther away from him, his hand snaked around her wrist and pulled her back.

"Lots and lots of them?"

"I shouldn't—"

"No, you shouldn't have— I don't like being compared unfavorably to other men. Maybe it's time I showed you just how talented I am in bed! You want to get over your hang-ups— Well, I'm just the guy to help you with that project!"

Her head thrashed from side to side, as he pulled her back down. Her skin was hot, and she trembled as if a fever raced through her senses. With one hand he gripped both wrists.

"First you ravaged me. Now I'll ravage you. Isn't this what you came over here for?"

"No." Tears slipped through her lashes.

"I don't believe you, darlin'."

With his free hand he traced a downward path over her breasts, lingering there till her nipples peaked. "You like being held down, don't you?"

She shuddered. When he laughed at her quick response, she kicked at him.

To no avail. He shifted his weight and overpowered her easily. "Your short skirt is definitely a plus."

She squirmed to escape him, but his fingers slid up her leg to that dewy place between her thighs. When he caressed her there, his fingers gentled. She caught her breath and then shivered when the finger probed deeper.

Underneath lime-green panties, she was wet. Hot. He couldn't believe it when he met virginal resistance, and the truth hit him.

She had hang-ups. She was scared. But she'd come to him. This was her first time. And he was scaring her again.

"There weren't any other men—"

"L-let me go," she murmured in broken whispers.

He was so nonplussed, he accidentally loosened his grip on her hands, and she pushed at him and somehow got away.

In a flash she shoved free and was out of bed and deftly rearranging her clothes and then running from him.

He got up and stormed after her. "Damn it, I wasn't trying to scare you!"

"I'm not scared! Not anymore! And you'd better not chase me outside, North Black—'cause you're stark naked!"

"So the hell what?"

So what if she was dressed and he wasn't?

"I'll call 911!"

Only when he heard one of his neighbor's cars outside, did he go back for his jeans.

Before he knew it, she was out of the bedroom. He heard his truck keys jingle in the living room.

"Not my truck!" he yelled. "Don't you dare drive my truck!"

His front door slammed. Footsteps raced down the front stairs.

He was yanking on his jeans and hopping toward the front door when she revved his truck loud enough to wake the whole complex. Bare-chested and barefooted, he was skidding down the concrete steps, shouting her name when she roared out of his parking lot so fast he smelled rubber.

"Those are brand-new tires, Melody! And my gun—"

She threw back her head triumphantly.

Behind him the wind caught his front door and slammed it shut.

"My! My! Mr. Black! That pretty girl is mad at you!" Mrs. Carey, his primmest old lady neighbor, who lived right below him, whom he'd long suspected had an innocent, girlish crush on him, got out of her Cadillac and beamed up at him.

A light went on in Mrs. Cullpepper's upstairs apartment. Damn.

He smiled at the blue-haired Mrs. Carey charmingly.

"Where's your shirt, Mr. Black?"

"Never mind." But his grin tightened.

When at last she headed for her door, he raced back upstairs. He twisted the knob of his apartment, but it was

locked. Even before he knelt to dig his key out of the flowerpot, he remembered Melody had taken his spare key inside.

"Damn. Damn."

"Is anything wrong up there, Mr. Black?"

"Couldn't be better," he hollered. "Good night, Mrs.
Carey."

He waited for the old dear to get inside. Only then did
he pick up the flowerpot and shake black dirt onto the
breezeway. With a weary sigh, he heaved his pot against
the window and then stepped back to avoid the spray of
glass and terra-cotta.

But a shard sliced his heel and got him yelping and hopping until he pulled it out and remembered the day he'd
stepped on a fishhook.

*Smile. It's the second best thing you can do with your
lips.*

And he did smile as he remembered Melody's velvet
tongue moving back and forth at his groin, her mouth hot,
probing, tantalizing him.

She'd been so silky and warm afterward.

Until he'd lost it. And scared her again.

Still, for once she'd certainly followed through. Had she
enjoyed it at all? Would she ever be willing to do it again?

Never, ever had he felt anything so pleasurable as her
hands and her mouth on his skin. He wasn't through with
the impossible Melody Woods after all.

Not by a long shot.

Six

Cathy's house seemed strange and mysterious in the dark with its roof splotched in purple shadows and bits of dazzling white.

Nervy and scared, Melody jumped back every time the pebbles she pitched pattered against the windowpane like shotgun pellets.

"Wake up, Cathy," Melody whispered, hunkering lower in the black hedge outside her friend's curtained window.

Nothing.

Melody's slim fingers fidgeted with the pebbles she held again, causing them to rattle. Again, her gaze swept the lawn to see if anyone was watching her. Above, leaves rustled in the heavy humid wind. She felt the breeze against her hot face. Other than the trees' noise and the distant whir of traffic on some thoroughfare, the neighborhood houses on Cathy's street were dark and silent.

Grimacing, Melody pinged several more handfuls against her friend's window. When still Cathy didn't answer, she raided the flower beds for more. Finally Melody picked up two handfuls and moved closer. When she arched her arms, rocks cracked against the glass.

The curtains were torn apart. The small window burst open, and Cathy's spiked head peeped cautiously above the straggling geraniums in her window box.

"Greg?"

"It's me—Melody."

Cathy's fingertips fluttered and were gone. She reappeared within seconds at her front door.

"I was asleep."

"You've got to help me."

Cathy stared at her blankly.

"This is all your fault you know."

"What on earth are you talking about?"

Melody turned away. "I—I… It's all so embarrassing. I—I stole North's truck. I've got to take it back. I can't see him or talk to him ever again. You've got to follow me in your car—"

"Okay. Okay. Give me a minute."

Five minutes later Cathy reappeared at the door again in shorts and a sweatshirt. She had her car keys in one hand and dangled her square little sparkly purse from the other. "So, how was it?"

Blushing, Melody raced down the front steps. "We'd better hurry—"

Cathy swung the purse back and forth. "You did it, didn't you? You finally had sex?"

"No!" She hesitated. "Well, sort of."

"Sort of?"

"I can't talk about it." How did other girls chatter about something so…so personal?

"You and North. Sort of." Cathy laughed. "That's great, babe. That's just great."

"Great?" They had reached North's white pickup. "It was awful. There is no me and North."

"How come you're in his truck then? You took a cab over there, didn't you? What happened?"

For no reason at all Melody was remembering how bronzed and gorgeous North had been against the tumble of white sheets. And how virile—so broad and brown and muscular at his shoulders, so lean at the waist and narrow at the hips. His legs had been paler. But they had been long and thick with muscle.

Melody blushed.

Cathy shrugged. "Babe, the first time's always the hardest. You'll like it. You'll get used to each other. I promise."

Used to each other? He'd been so furious. She'd felt so hurt. Even now Melody still felt vulnerable, raw, too easy to read—and so out there. "You don't understand," she mumbled.

"Oh, but I do. Trust me. This is going to be wonderful."

"Oh, Cathy—"

"No regrets, okay? Remember that pact we made when you broke up with North last time? We're going to be women of power. We're going to live and do our own thing, just like men do. We're going to know who we are and what we want and we're going to be equal to any man. And that means no regrets. North's a great guy, and you're a great gir...er...woman. This is a win-win, babe."

"It sounds so simple in theory."

"Babe, it's way more fun in reality."

The sea breeze that had roared all night was still gusting in the early-morning dark. Out to the southwest, the clouds were black.

Inside, North tugged a tall black boot on, cursing it until it slid over his heel. Next he tore a shirt off a hanger and pulled it on.

Even though he was in town, even though he hadn't gotten much sleep, he was a man of regular habits. Thus, he was up as early as ever. Although the pleasant aroma of bacon and coffee lingered in his apartment, he'd eaten and had coffee and stuffed the dishwasher over an hour ago.

Was it the city or Melody that had him as edgy as a wild bronc that didn't want to be broken? Melody—for sure.

The white walls of the boxy room seemed to close in on him as he crammed his crisp white shirt into his jeans. For a long moment he stared at his rumpled bed and wished Melody were still there, asleep in his bed, her cheeks rosily aglow. He wished he hadn't pushed, hadn't thought, hadn't started one of their quarrels—hadn't scared her.

What she'd done to him had been a soul-stealing pleasure. He wished he could hold her and kiss her and cuddle close to her till she woke up.

If she had to run out, he was almost glad she'd run off in his truck. It gave him an excuse to go after her.

He picked up the phone. He would've called her first thing, if he'd been sure where she was—at her parents' or her grandmother's. He glanced at his watch. It was still too early to call her at the Woodses', so he dialed Jeff.

He would have preferred not to call Jeff. He wasn't in the mood to deal with his cattle buyer or accountant, either. He wanted his mind to settle down, and for that to happen, he needed to talk to Melody.

But if he didn't call Jeff, Jeff would suspect something. No matter where North was, they always hashed out the ranch work schedule together.

"So—was Melody there last night?" Jeff demanded in a surly tone right after he said hello.

"My life is not some soap opera you can tune into at will. Who you got doing fence in the La Negra division down south?"

"Was the dinner just a ruse to set you up with Melody? I gotta know, buddy."

"She...er... That issue didn't come up," North lied smoothly. "Did you hear anything out of our Midnight Bandit?"

"That issue?" Jeff laughed. "That's a pretty borin' description of a mighty interestin', rabble-rousin' little gal."

"You finished, Mr. Gossip-monger?"

"If you're done with her, can I date her?"

"Shut the hell up!"

"Touch-e-e-e," Jeff drawled. "I wouldn't touch that one with a ten-foot pole."

"Not that you've got one."

"Don't be cruel." Jeff laughed and finished knowingly, "So the issue didn't come up."

"Confound it, Gentry! How the hell's Little Camel?"

"You need to get yourself laid. The sooner the better. Good thing we've got hot dates with Maria and Tina."

"Maria?"

"Saturday, remember?"

"I'm beat. Can I get out of that—"

"So the issue did make an appearance."

North said nothing. When they were done talking llamas, bandits, stretchers, wire, posts and pliers, North kept his voice deliberately casual. "One more thing. Could you call my apartment manager over here? Somebody broke my window last night."

"Did you call the police?"

"Just get him to fix it. Tell him it's on me."

"Now that sounds... What the hell did she do—"

"Get off her, understand! Good thing you're not standing here, or you wouldn't still be standing."

"Hey, I almost forgot. W.T. was burning needles off prickly pears with a butane torch and damned if that slacker didn't set half the north pasture on fire."

North tensed.

"Got it out. Not much damage. A few fence stakes. That's all. Got a little rain, too. Might get more."

"Hey. I saw some clouds this morning. Wow."

When a car honked downstairs, North strode to the front window.

"My cab's here."

"What's wrong with your truck?"

"Gotta go." North was halfway down the outside stairs before he realized the cab was parked right beside a white truck.

His pickup.

"Damn your hide, darlin'. You ran out on me again."

He paid the driver with two crisp ten-dollar bills. Then as a matter of course he walked around his truck inspecting it for new dings, checking the tires, too.

She'd left the windows open. His keys were dangling from the ignition. Anybody could have taken it.

Then he remembered his daddy's Colt.

Couldn't she ever do one thing right?

Smile. It's the second best thing you can do with your lips.

Oh, yeah, she could.

North jumped inside and yanked his glove box open. When his hand closed over the carved leather holster, he breathed a sigh of relief. The holster had been his father's. The Colt had been a gift from him on that last birthday before—

North turned it over and over before replacing it inside the glove box. Then he sat in his truck for a long time. Maybe it was W.T. starting the fire that got him thinking about his father. Maybe Melody had him feeling more vulnerable.

His daddy, Rand Black, had been a real, bigger-than-life cowboy hero. He'd expanded the ranch's acreage, negotiated favorable oil leases and crossbred cattle until he'd come up with a superior breed. He'd been an inventor and a national celebrity—and those accomplishments had only been the beginning.

North had wanted to be just like him when he grew up. Then, shortly after North's twelfth birthday, his father had been killed in a fire that had started in some stacks of wood and then had spread to the barn. His father's office had been in the loft. Nobody knew he was missing until the fire was out.

Gran always said North was Rand's spitting image, that she'd never known a son to be so like his father.

Naturally North's mother, Anne, who'd never had the most harmonious of relationships with her husband or mother-in-law, had disagreed. "Rand wasn't a god."

"In these parts he was," Gran always countered.

"He was mortal. Now he's dead," his mother always persisted.

"He was the most popular person on this ranch. And North is going to be just like him."

"Nobody should have to live up to a legend."

"Is that why you didn't shed a tear at the funeral?"

"I run off, as you put it, because I'm alive and Rand's dead, and I don't want to go out of my mind."

His mother had done her maternal duty. Two years ago on one of her trips to Paris, she'd fallen in love.

North hadn't wanted her to tell him about her German count. On her last visit, which had been short and tense, she had told him anyway.

"I want to visit your father's grave before I go," she'd said that last day.

"Why?"

"Maybe to reassure myself his name is really on the tombstone."

"Are you going to marry your count?"

She'd arched a thin, black eyebrow that was many shades darker than her fluffy bright hair. "No."

"How could you be with somebody else—after him?"

"I'm alive. Rand is dead." She'd knelt before his tombstone and traced the letters of his name. "Really really dead." She'd looked up at North. "For years I lived in his shadow. And then for years I lived here in the shadow of his legend. Everything had to be done according to his wishes."

"He was a great rancher."

"You can't hold back change, North." She'd laid a single red rose on the grave and got up. "Not even in a feudal kingdom like El Dorado. He's gone. Let him go."

"That's easy for you to say."

"Oh, no. You don't know how wrong you are. Don't waste your life the way I wasted mine."

It was sunny when Melody awoke. She'd fallen asleep on the edge of the bed beside her teddy bears and on top of her red spread.

Rubbing her eyes, she realized she was exhausted in body and mind. Her mouth was dry, and she had a headache. At first she was so disoriented, she didn't know what was wrong. Then the memory of what she'd done last night and what North had thought of her afterward hit her smack-dab in the middle of her forehead.

Her cheeks got so hot, she was probably purple. Slowly, avoiding looking at herself in her long mirror, she got out of bed and ran to her bathroom.

Splashing hot water onto her face, she scrubbed and scrubbed. Next she brushed her teeth and then drank a long glass of water. Only when her mouth was all minty and clean did she look in the mirror. Other than the telltale color of her cheeks, her face was as angelic and innocent looking as ever.

Last night had left no visible trace.

Except for North, nobody knew.

Who taught you?

She had a few days before her classes started. Maybe she should hide out in Austin.

She was wondering what to do when her phone rang.

It was exactly nine o'clock.

North never called her at her parents' before that hour. Even before she crossed the room and read his name on the caller ID, her heart was already racing.

More than anything she wanted to talk to him. But she was too scared of what she'd done and he'd said.

Would he apologize? Or would he condemn her? She touched the receiver with trembling fingertips and then jumped back every time it rang.

On the fifth ring she picked it up.

"Melody—"

She lost her nerve and hung up on him.

When it rang again, she picked it up and laid it on her bed. Then she ran outside and buried her face in her hands. After she'd finished loving him last night, she'd lifted her head. She felt breathily on fire when his dark eyes had glinted as he'd stared into hers and then down her body. Terrified, she'd been in heaven and hell when he'd pulled her closer, caressing her temples, his gentle fingertips moving in slow, hypnotic circles.

Ablaze with incomprehensible tenderness and passion and yet fear, too, she'd touched her lips with the back of her hand in wonder, and he'd taken that hand and brought it to his lips. He'd kissed each fingertip, and then he'd kissed her.

He'd wanted more. He'd been gentle, but suddenly her old fears had mushroomed, and she'd buried her face in his throat and held onto him fiercely. And all the while some wanton part of her had secretly craved him.

Why had he gotten so angry? Did he think she was cheap now? He must. She tried to remember every detail, so she could understand. But it was all so new to her, so baffling—so terrible.

"Look at me, little darlin'," he'd whispered, lifting her chin.

She'd shut her eyes.

"You want more. Same as I do."

She'd shaken her head.

As they lain in the dark, his arms around her, she'd felt him gradually tense. When he'd let her go and cursed her and accused her of sleeping with other men, she'd been truly mortified.

You've got quite a knack for it, darlin'.

His face had been so stern and unforgiving, she'd been sure he despised her. Her heart had begun to beat with terror. Hardly knowing what she said, she'd lashed out, too.

Then he'd grabbed her, and low, wicked creature that she was, she'd reveled when he'd said, "Now I'll ravage you."

Oh, dear! She was even worse than he thought she was. In the blazing sunshine, it all seemed so cheap and sordid. And yet...

Last night when he'd tackled her with that voracious hunger, she'd felt so turned on, she could have abandoned a lifetime of inhibitions.

This morning she had a hangover. That was a first, too.

She couldn't face him ever again. As she stepped back into her room, she heard her mother's shrill voice from the hall.

The door opened.

"You could knock—"

"Sorry. Why in the world do you have the phone off the hook?"

"Um...er..."

Dee Dee's eyes moved over Melody in that comprehensive nosy manner all mothers have down to a T. "Darling, what's wrong? You're as white as a sheet."

Melody forced a valiant smile. "Nothing."

"Homesick?"

"I'm fine."

Dee Dee's face grew taut. "All right. If you say so. You get dressed, and I'll fix you a great big omelet. Vegetarian."

"Thank you, Mother."

Dee Dee set the phone on the hook. It rang before she could get out the door.

Melody stared at it. "Don't answer it!"

"But I'm the hostess of that charity ball."

Before Melody could stop her, Dee Dee had picked up the phone. "Why...hello, North..."

"I'm not here," Melody mouthed silently, shaking her head. "I won't talk to him."

All of a sudden Dee Dee saw way too much. "Uh...no... She's...she's not here. Uh...maybe...maybe she went out to the university to see about her classes or over to Nana's to work out her move.... Yes. I'll tell her. It was great seeing you, too, last night, dear."

Dee Dee hung up. "What is going on?"

"Nothing," Melody answered quietly.

Dee Dee stared.

"Nothing! And...and I want to keep it that way."

"Do you have to be rude to him?"

"Yes. Mother, please—"

Dee Dee watched her daughter for a very long moment. "I will never understand you."

Seven

The whole thing happened so quickly.

It seemed to Melody she'd been stuck behind the armored Dodge truck with the tinted windows going twenty, stewing over North for hours. Then something moved in the tangles of brush along the side of the road, and instantly the brake lights in front of her blazed red.

The Dodge pulled over and stopped so abruptly, she nearly rammed it. As she passed the monstrous SUV, half a dozen uniformed men swarmed out and chased running figures through the thorny mesquite.

She was so upset, she didn't really register what the high drama was all about. Her head ached as she remembered all the things North had patiently explained to her about his home and his land the first and only time he'd brought her here to meet his family.

The thick brush was problematic because livestock could hide in it, but it was a paradise for wildlife—for Nilgai antelope, quail, feral hogs, and of course, white-tailed deer.

PLAY THE
Lucky Key Game
and get

HOW TO PLAY:

1. With a coin, carefully scratch off gold area at the right. Then check the claim chart to see what we have for you — **2 FREE BOOKS** and a **FREE GIFT** — **ALL YOURS FREE!**

2. Send back the card and you'll receive two brand-new Silhouette Desire® novels. These books have a cover price of $3.99 each in the U.S. and $4.50 each in Canada, but they are yours to keep absolutely free.

3. There's no catch. You're under no obligation to buy anything. We charge nothing —ZERO — for your first shipment. And you don't have to make any minimum number of purchases — not even one!

4. The fact is, thousands of readers enjoy receiving books by mail from the Silhouette Reader Service™. They enjoy the convenience of home delivery...they like getting the best new novels at discount prices, BEFORE they're available in stores...and they love their *Heart to Heart* subscriber newsletter featuring author news, horoscopes, recipes, book reviews and much more!

5. We hope that after receiving your free books you'll want to remain a subscriber. But the choice is yours — to continue or cancel, any time at all! So why not take us up on our invitation, with no risk of any kind. You'll be glad you did!

YOURS FREE!
A SURPRISE MYSTERY GIFT

We can't tell you what it is...but we're sure you'll like it! A
FREE GIFT—
just for playing the
LUCKY KEY game!

Visit us online at
www.eHarlequin.com

FREE GIFTS!

NO COST! NO OBLIGATION TO BUY!
NO PURCHASE NECESSARY!

PLAY THE
Lucky Key Game

Scratch gold area with a coin.
Then check below to see the gifts you get!

326 SDL DC64
225 SDL DC6Y

YES! I have scratched off the gold area. Please send me the 2 Free books and gift for which I qualify. I understand I am under no obligation to purchase any books, as explained on the back and on the opposite page.

NAME   (PLEASE PRINT CLEARLY)

ADDRESS

APT.#   CITY

STATE/PROV.   ZIP/POSTAL CODE

2 free books plus a mystery gift	1 free book
2 free books	Try Again!

Offer limited to one per household and not valid to current
Silhouette Desire® subscribers. All orders subject to approval.

(S-D-OS-07/01)

The Silhouette Reader Service™ — Here's how it works:

"Which you keep to kill," she'd said.

"Hunting is an important economic factor in managing El Dorado."

"This is the twenty-first century. Hunting is barbaric."

"City girl…"

"I can't help what I am."

"Neither can I."

She was crazy to come back to Bertie's feudal kingdom.

Suddenly she realized what the big Dodge meant—the Border Patrol was out in force flushing illegal aliens.

She swallowed as she thought of the poor countries she'd visited and the desperate lives she'd witnessed. India and China were a whole lot worse than Mexico. Still, during college she'd spent enough weekends and summers in Mexico translating for an American doctor friend of her father's, who ran a free clinic. The poor patients had been crushingly poor. So poor, Melody was familiar with the raw smell of armpits and feet, of bad teeth and dirty clothes. The patients had wheedled, their voices demanding, obscene, angry, friendly. She'd known that no matter what she gave them, it wasn't enough.

The private narrow ranch road that led to El Dorado's headquarters was ten miles long and lined on both sides with tall palms. Their black shadows were bars of darkness.

Melody turned the volume up. Now that she was past the Dodge, she was driving way too fast again and playing her tape too loud. But that was just because she was so nervous. Even though her fingertips kept time and she was humming, she wasn't really listening to the music. All of a sudden she was remembering that one disastrous weekend she'd spent here.

The big house had been filled with snooty, out-of-town relatives along with a senator who'd been flown in by private jet all the way from Washington D.C. She'd gotten so scared she'd forgotten to change shoes and had come down to dinner in a formal and jogging shoes. When everybody had laughed, and North had suggested she go back upstairs and change, she'd gotten defensive and had pretended she'd chosen the outfit deliberately.

Always, always, who North was had gotten in her way. He was so rich, so big, at least in south Texas. Why, his daddy had been as famous as a movie star.

She hadn't really realized until that weekend that dating North was like dating royalty, that if she married him she would never again be free to just be who she was, whoever Melody Woods was.

Maybe he lived in an isolated ranch house in the middle of nowhere, but when she'd met those people, she'd known that he belonged to a glittering world that was beyond her and above her. When he went to Europe, he played polo with princes. Naturally her socially ambitious mother had been wild for her to marry him.

"You'll get used to it, grow into it. Besides, most of the time, you'll be on the ranch."

"Which is boring. I don't care that he has miles and miles of tight fences or all those thousands of cows he's so proud of."

His family had thought she was as ambitious as her mother, that she was marrying him for who he was and what he had, when those were the very things she'd held against him.

"I know you're not like your mother," North had said to reassure her when she hadn't wanted to wear that huge, ancestral diamond he'd given her for an engagement ring.

"Can't I have a little diamond…one that you bought just for me?" she'd begged.

"That wouldn't be right."

In the end he and Libby, his grandmother, had been offended because she'd so rarely worn his ring.

A wild turkey raced across the road. Melody hit the brakes and then smiled as she waited. The big bird, head bobbing, danced about in zigzagging circles. Finally it took off, flapping clumsily over the fence, vanishing into the thick mesquite brush.

Cathy had put her up to this venture with more of her crazy sex advice when she'd dropped by to swim earlier this afternoon.

They'd lain in the shade by the pool together and sipped lemonade.

"Is your daddy home, babe? Can I take off my top and toast all over?"

"No. And no. Mother would have a fit."

"I've never seen you so glum. You really want Bertie, babe?"

"He's arrogant and..."

"But you want him.... So—go get him."

"What? He's at his ranch. They call him 'King' there. Jeff says he's busy and doesn't want to talk to me."

"So—you've called the ranch?" Cathy remarked dryly.

Behind her sunglasses, Melody had squinched her eyes shut.

"You've got wheels, babe."

"I can't just chase him."

"Who said chase? He won't speak to you?" Cathy sucked the last of her lemonade and grinned. "Give him hell."

"I don't get you."

Cathy ran a fingertip up her wet, cold glass and then licked the condensation off it with lascivious show of pink tongue. "Trust me," she said huskily. "Guys love a change of pace."

"I can't stand the country. It is so boring."

"Think of it as one of your adventures...like a safari or something. Melody's cowgirl adventure."

"Cowgirl, my eye. I fell off a horse the last time I was there! The saddle slipped or something. North got real mad at Jeff later. Said he tied the cinch knot all wrong."

"On purpose?"

"I'm not sure. He doesn't like me. Anyway, when I tried to right myself, I jammed my foot all the way through my stirrup. The horse was going so fast, and I was trapped down between her legs. I got skinned on one side.''

''Oh—''

''Then North jumped in front of the horse and grabbed the reins. He saved my life.''

''Well, just remember the only animal down there you're going to climb on and ride is your hero, King Bertie!''

''You're incorrigible!''

''If you get bored on that ranch with Bertie, it's your fault. Hook him big time!''

So, here Melody was, driving toward North's house like a love-struck fool. This thought was cut off when she saw the ranch's white gatehouse up ahead and the letters that spelled El Dorado shimmering in heat waves.

She tensed when she saw the man inside the little house. Then she realized she was in luck. The gate was wide-open.

As soon as he saw her, the slim, rangy gatekeeper set his Stetson straight, pushed his sunglasses higher, and shoved whatever he was reading under the counter. Pasting on what he supposed was a super-sexy smile, he hopped out of his boxy shack square in the middle of the road. Square in front of her.

His red, mirrored sunglasses so startled Melody, she slammed on the brakes.

Tires shrieked.

''Hey, hey, watch where you're going, Miss…Woods….''

Melody lowered her window and rapped her fingers on her steering wheel in high agitation and stared anywhere but at him.

The un-air-conditioned heat rose from the asphalt like a furnace blast.

''I just bet you've got the prettiest eyes,'' she said, ''under those awful glasses.''

Grinning at her, he removed the offending glasses, and she relaxed a little.

"You're famous around here," he said, "or should I say, notorious? Pretty in pink, too."

Melody burned as if the skin over her heart was emblazoned with a scarlet letter *A*. Had North told every yokel on the ranch he'd scored?

"Notorious?" She licked her lips. "That's a mighty big word for a little boy who wastes his time reading dirty comics."

He flared instantly. "How'd— I wasn't—"

"You hid that comic book mighty fast. Lemme see."

He blushed tellingly.

"Thought so." She laughed with a great deal more confidence than she felt.

The sun was brilliant. Even though she wasn't wearing all that much—a pink, sleeveless knit top, matching pink shorts that didn't quite meet in the middle—and her window was down, she would still soon be sweltering. If only he'd move a little more to the left—

"How in the world do those black cows over there stand this?"

A rivulet of sweat ran down his smooth cheek. "I've got orders not to let you in, Miss Woods."

"Then I guess we'll just have to get acquainted—handsome."

His eyebrows lifted. Through her windshield, his gaze drilled her belly button. "You are certainly living up to your reputation."

"I'll take that as a compliment."

He was gorgeous, too gorgeous for his own good. Not that his babyish golden looks appealed to her. His heavy eyelids lowered to half-mast and stayed there, giving him a sleepy, rather worthless look.

"Poor boy. You look dog-tired out here in this heat," she said. "We're going to have to think of something to perk you up."

"I know just the thing." Full of confidence, he swaggered around to her door.

Finally. "Cute shorts—"

Men were so hopeful. It was part of their charm.

She hit the accelerator.

"Hey!"

Tires squealed. Melody stopped a safe distance down the road to gloat a little. "You're not too good at your job are you?"

"Now you come back here."

"And you don't know too much about women, either. You keep reading those books. Maybe you'll learn something. And, handsome. Count yourself lucky you're not roadkill. Don't you ever, ever jump in front of another lady's car, understand? She might not be as good a driver as me. Oh! I nearly forgot. You call your boss. You tell King Bertie he's got company."

The boy's lips thinned as he glanced worriedly around. "The king's not gonna like this." He slid his sunglasses back on.

"Then I'll have to put in a good word for you. What's your name?"

"W.T."

Melody laughed and then tromped the pedal with her toe again.

Better to laugh than to give in to her fear or cry.

Melody jumped. There it was again—the sound. The faint creaking of a board in the loft or the crackle of hay under a hoof.

How could a big empty barn seem scary?

Because she was a city girl, out of her element.

A slight moan, high in the eaves. Suddenly she felt so vulnerable, so alone in the big barn as she explored, cracking stall doors and peering into them at the cows and their newborns.

Hot little prickles of alarm raced down her spine. She threw an uneasy glance toward the loft. Was somebody watching her? Or was she just so nervous—

As scared as a little kid, she shut the stall door with trembling hands. After that afternoon when those boys had caught her, she used to lie in her bed every night, sure that something evil lurked in the dark. Sometimes, it didn't take much for those old fears to take over.

She scanned the length of the barn—nothing. Still, she had to fight the urge to run. The house, Sissy, and his grandmother had been bad enough.

The barn, even alone, should be easier.

She pushed another stall door open anyway.

At last, llamas!

She smiled. "Hi, guys—"

Two pairs of soft brown eyes stared uncertainly into hers.

"Don't be afraid." Still shaking, she marched into the llamas' stall as brazenly as she'd stomped across the lush green lawn up to the big house where she'd paused to admire Libby Black's pink oleander and white jimson weed blossoms before knocking on the big front door.

The old lady, her thin mouth agape, had come out on the porch in her big straw hat, muddy boots, holding a tall glass of iced tea.

"Hello?" they'd both said at once.

Then Melody had asked, "How in the world do you make the desert bloom like this, Mrs. Black?"

"Lots of water and two good cowboys." The old lady had frowned. "North didn't tell me you were coming."

"Didn't know I was till I got here. Would you please tell him I'm here?"

"Oh, dear," Sissy had come outside then, her dark, angelic face, concerned. "North has been an absolute bear ever since he got home from Corpus. He didn't tell us you...and he even saw each other."

"Could I see him, please—"

"He's..." Sissy's dark brows had knitted. "We've had a little..." Libby had given her a warning look. "It's nothing really.... Just some trouble."

"He's okay?"

Sissy had nodded. "Our pilot flew him down to the border. Five miles of good fence with fresh holes cut in it. A truck stolen. Missing cattle. He's down there riding fence—"

"Then I'll wait."

"No telling how long he'll be really," Sissy had said.

"How about a glass of tea?" Libby had offered.

The baby llama moved hesitantly toward Melody. When the animal nuzzled her belly button with a warm wet nose, she laughed out loud. "I bet you're thirsty."

Sissy had said there was a refrigerator in the tack room and that she could feed Little Camel while she waited. When Melody left the stall, she heard that same eerie sound echoing in the rafters again.

She stopped, waiting. The barn seemed huge and darker than before. All of a sudden she remembered Rand Black had died in the barn. Her eyes ran over the fifty pound sacks of feed, halters, bridles and saddles.

Not this barn! The other one had been a total loss.

The wood of the stalls glowed a pretty shade of red in the late-evening light. Even though it was late, it was still hot. Melody had been wandering around inside the large building less than half an hour, and already the lingering heat and fierce humidity had her pink knit top plastered to her spine and breasts. Her linen shorts felt limp. The hot, stifling air reeked of horses, feed and leather.

When something big began to stomp and snort and bray in another stall, she nearly jumped out of her skin. She almost wished she were back in the parlor trying to make awkward conversation with Sissy and Libby.

The tack room was at the far end of the barn. She saw North's father's name cut into the door. North had told her all the cowboys had carved their names on the door. Right under Rand's name, North had carved his own. Then she saw Jeff's. Even that lazy W.T. had taken the time to carve his. She was tracing the letters of North's name, when she heard a boot heel again—nearer. Someone else really was in the barn. No ghost! But someone sneaky who didn't want her to know he was there.

Something soft wrapped around her leg.

She screamed, and then sank to her knees laughing when she saw it was only a rotund ginger cat. He began to meow loudly. Swishing his tail, he evaded her outstretched hand and stalked stiffly toward the refrigerator.

"Oh, so you want some milk, too?"

Another demanding yowl.

Not that the yellow monster deigned to turn and glance at her.

She opened the refrigerator. Mr. Ginger swirled around her legs, as she lifted the milk carton. Then the boot heel rang on concrete again, and a deep voice behind her said her name.

"Melody!"

Startled, she peered out the door into the dark barn but saw nothing. No one.

Forgetting the cat and the llamas, she stepped out of the tack room into the darkening barn.

"Who is it?" she whispered.

Still nothing.

She heard a footfall behind her and before fear could spiral through her, she whirled.

Two long shadows covered hers. Two men, one lean and rangy wearing a Stetson; the other burly, his baseball cap turned backward, stared at her. No more than twenty feet away, they seemed to have materialized out of thin air.

"You'd better git, girl. King don't want nothin' to do with you," said the one in the baseball hat.

The light came from behind them, so she couldn't see their faces.

"Jeff?"

"I told you, it was her, Gentry!" said the kid from the gate. "You shouldn't have taken off like that, Miss

Woods," he purred, shifting his weight from one high-heeled boot to the other.

"W.T. and me—we got better things to do than play cat and mouse with a troublemaker like you."

They were both wearing mirrored sunglasses as they stalked her.

"You never did like me, did you, Jeff?" she whispered.

The two men exchanged a look.

"You're trespassing, Pinky Pooh," Jeff answered.

When she saw four tiny blondes in pink reflected back at her, dread washed over her. It was almost as if she was that terrified little girl again, and those four boys were chasing her.

She couldn't seem to focus on anything other than their shadowy faces and those sunglasses. "You stay away from me."

W.T. laughed, but his eyes bored through her. "You ain't so sassy now."

Prickles of alarm traced up her spine again. All she knew was that she had to get out of the dark barn and away from them. In her panic, she pivoted too sharply. When she ran, they took off after her. She stumbled over a rake. Then the milk carton slid through her fingers and splashed onto the concrete floor.

She stepped in it and slid, falling, hitting the concrete on outstretched palms so hard, it knocked the breath out of her.

They were leaning down, their brawny arms reaching for her. Blood pounded in her temples.

Then barn doors rolled apart noisily, and more vivid red sunlight exploded behind a tall broad-shouldered man with a gun strapped to his right hip.

There were three of them. She was outnumbered. Like before when she'd been eleven. She started screaming.

"Gentry, W.T., just what the hell is going on?" a deep, familiar voice yelled.

"Bertie," Melody gasped weakly. "Bertie..."

He'd come, just in time, again.

"She fell, King," Jeff said. "I swear. That's all—"

North's heavy boot heels resounded on the concrete, echoing all the way to the rafters as he loped toward her.

"Gran just told me she needs two big boys on that front bed. You two git!" His lazy drawl held an edge of menace.

The two demoted cowboys stayed put and said, "We weren't doing nothin' to her. She was trespassing."

"Git! I said!" North repeated, again, in *that* voice they knew and feared.

When at last they skulked past her out of the barn, North took Melody's hand and helped her up. "My big bozos scare you, did they?"

Staring at his gun, she shook her head. If she admitted the truth, then they would dislike her even more for getting them into trouble.

"And no wonder—they're both as ugly as all get out, aren't they?" he murmured.

She drew a deep breath. "It was a simple misunderstanding."

"So—you're okay?"

Her right knee and her left hand throbbed. She was still too stunned to answer. Embarrassed, she threw herself against him and held on tightly. "I—I didn't mean to cause you any trouble."

He was so tall and strong. He felt good, she clung, burying her nose into his cotton shirt so deeply she got a whiff of laundry detergent along with his own fresh male odor. And that made her remember how he'd tasted, which instantly caused thrilling little jolts of male-female awareness to sizzle through her.

He held her stiffly. She drew back, feeling ashamed of what she'd done the other night all over again. For a long moment, the silence that stretched between them seemed as taut as her nerves.

"I wasn't trespassing," she whispered. "I came to see you."

He frowned. "You're always welcome here, Melody. I told you that."

"I—I just wanted to talk to you. I—I tried and tried... Why...why are you wearing that gun?"

"We've had a little excitement around here. I wear it when I'm out alone. Nothing for you to be scared of. I'm sorry I've been kind of hard to reach." He brushed a loose strand of hair from her cheek and cupped her chin as if to lift her lips to his. "What do you need? You've got my full attention now."

She licked her lips.

His gaze narrowed, and he studied her mouth so lingeringly her heartbeats began to quicken. "What was so all-fired important—"

"You know the other night..."

"Oh, yeah," he breathed. "I called you to say I was sorry and you hung up on me."

"I came out to tell you... About all those other men... I'm sorry, too. There weren't any. I mean I lied when I said there were lots and lots.... I—I really didn't know what I was doing when I kissed you like that. I—I was just following my instincts. If I seemed like I knew what I was doing, I guess I just got carried away."

He stared at her in wonder and confusion. "My God, Melody—"

"North?" floated a silken feminine voice behind them.

At the note of possession in that third voice, North moved, uneasily shifting his weight from one foot to the other. "Damn." There was guilt in his low tone.

Melody jumped away from him.

"What's going on?" the newcomer asked very sweetly.

"She's had a little scare, that's all," North explained a little too awkwardly.

Obviously he had a date with Maria. He'd invited Maria, who was perfect for him, here tonight. Not her. He'd gone from her to—

Of all the miserable, rotten, bad timing...!

Afraid she might cry, which would never do, Melody raised her head and wiped at her eyes.

The dark girl, who stood in the last of the red sunlight, was staring at North as if she owned him. And maybe she did now.

Why, oh why, did Maria have to be as dazzlingly beautiful in her tight jeans and cowboy hat as her own sister Claire? Only Claire was blond while this young woman with the hourglass figure had soft, inky waves of black hair and big black eyes that shone like buttons.

Had North ever made love to her?

"You must be Maria," Melody said, her voice strange and hoarse, not her own.

"This is Melody...Woods, an old...friend."

"I know who she is." After a little awkward interval, Maria smiled. "I don't understand. What is she doing here?"

Suddenly Melody realized she was the intruder, not Maria. Jeff had just been trying to warn her a few minutes ago, so she'd leave and save herself the embarrassment of this little scene.

She had to say something. "I—I was about to feed Little Camel while I waited for North."

"Her visit was probably impulsive," North said, protecting her. "And a surprise to me," he finished, protecting himself. "Would you give us a minute alone, Maria?"

"Sure."

"Why are you here?" he asked when Maria was outside with W.T. and Jeff.

"I—I don't guess it really matters now," Melody said, floundering helplessly. How could she say the things she wanted to say when three people lurked right outside the barn, trying to hear her every word.

"Clue me in for once—anyway."

"I told you I tried to call you to talk to you about—" She broke off. "Several times. Only Jeff wouldn't—"

"Gentry? He didn't tell me you called."

"It doesn't matter. I guess he knew how you felt."

"You're wrong."

"I don't believe you."

"Then maybe you'll believe him, darlin'." Before she could stop him, North called out to his friend. "Gentry, what's this about? Melody here says she called me, and you refused— Gentry!"

When Jeff didn't answer immediately, North repeated himself. "You answer me! I know you're out there snooping like usual."

Jeff stuck his bright red head inside the barn. "King, correct me if I'm wrong. So what if she called? You did say that as far as I was concerned, this little Woods gal no longer existed, am I right?"

North lowered his voice until it wasn't much more than a growl. "That's irrelevant...now," he said to Melody. "That was before—"

"Was it irrelevant? Or was it crazy of me to call you or come here? Crazy of me to think," Melody murmured. More upset than ever, she began backing away from him toward the door. "I see how things are. Forget..."

North grabbed her wrist. He seemed to be having a hard time breathing. "Melody, so help me if you run out on me one more time when we're in the middle of something—"

"It's over," she whispered. "I see that."

"You said I was the first."

"That doesn't matter now. But I'm glad I came. Glad I saw I was right about this place...and...and you. Glad I don't fit in—"

"Your impulsive mind works awful fast." He let her go, crossed his arms. He looked angry enough to explode all of a sudden. "Have you ever wanted to fit in?"

"No! Why would I? This is a tight little boring world. And you're—"

He stiffened. "Boring?" he finished helpfully.

The way he said it, in *that* voice, sent a thread of fear through her. "Yes. Yes. You think you're king here in this

macho kingdom of yours. You think you're safe because
life hasn't changed for a hundred years."

"What if I wasn't as boring as you're determined to
think I am? What then?"

She thought of how thrilled she'd felt in his apartment,
and a red flush stole up her slender throat and flamed her
cheeks.

"King, she said she wants to go," Jeff yelled.

"Shut up, Gentry!" To Melody, North said softly, "If
you'd stick around for once instead of always hightailin'
it, you might learn different."

North cast an uneasy glance at his men and Maria, who
were all glaring at Melody so mutinously from the opening
a few yards away, she felt most unwelcome.

"They don't like me," Melody whispered hoarsely.

"You've never given them a chance. You could start by
telling us what was so all-fired important to get you out
here?"

Again, she was in the bedroom of his apartment. Again
she was on his bed vividly responding to his lovemaking.
She'd just told him he was the only man she'd ever done
something like that with. How could she talk about any of
that now, under these circumstances?

"You big lug, if you really don't know, then you are a
real idiot!"

She dived past him and started running. She heard
North's shouts behind her.

"Hey, wait one cock-eyed minute!"

He sprinted after her. His men, their mirrored glasses
glittering, planted their long legs in front of the opening in
the barn, forming a human wall that barred her way.

When North caught up to her, she whirled, determined
to fight him, but his hard hands circled her slender waist
and held on tight. Crying out in dismay as he pulled her
closer, she pounded his muscular back.

"Just tell me, only me then," he repeated inexorably,

breathing hard, tugging her deeper into a private corner of the barn.

Stinging sweat—or was it tears?—dripped into her eyes. Furious, she wiped them away with the back of her hand.

"Why do you upset me so much?" she whispered.

"I don't know. You tell me."

"I lay awake all night long after what I—I did the other night—"

"So did I, darlin'."

"But why?'

"'Cause we liked it too much. 'Cause we want more. And it makes us sad and angry. 'Cause we know it can't ever work in the long run."

"Then please, if you know it won't work," she sobbed, "just let me go."

"Even now…when we both know it, that's not so easy, is it, darlin'?" Holding her frightened glance, he bent his lips to her ear and grinned when she jumped because the warmth of his breath tickled and gave her terrifying pleasure.

"You did come back for more even though you don't think it'll work out, didn't you?"

She sobbed quietly into his hard shoulder.

"Admit it, darlin'."

She shook her head.

"You want me to make love to you, don't you?" His callused fingers brushed the soft hair off her neckline. "I mean really make love. My lips doing all the things you did to me." Even his voice made her quiver. "We could do it just for fun. No strings attached."

"No."

"Would that be so terrible?" he demanded huskily.

"Yes. Yes."

"Yes, to terrible?"

He was holding her so tightly, her breath came unevenly, and she was beginning to tremble.

"Or yes to sex?" he persisted in a velvet, sensual tone that undid her.

She paused for what seemed like a lifetime, and he lifted her chin, as if he needed to read her expression. She was studying the cruelly beautiful shape of his mouth and half opening her own so that he could kiss her as she longed, when suddenly Jeff let out a war whoop and ran away from the barn toward the south pastures. There he began yelling loud enough to raise the next ranch house. Pistol raised, he fired a warning shot.

A horse neighed in the distance.

"Hot damn! If it ain't the Midnight Bandit!" W.T. hollered.

North and Melody shot out of the barn together.

Spurs jingling, a lone, mythical cowboy, whose skin glowed like copper, trotted toward them on a tall black horse. The rider sported a sweeping handlebar mustache and a strange, low-crowned hat.

North hadn't ever seen anyone quite like him. Automatically his right hand went to his gun.

"Don't you dare shoot at him!" Melody screamed, breaking free and running toward the stranger who seemed to float toward them on that magnificent animal in a shimmering haze of blinding red light.

"North, don't you see he's carrying a little boy in his arms?"

Eight

North's eyes narrowed on the stranger. Maybe because Melody was so fascinated by him, his own voice came out more curt than usual. "Can I help you, mister?"

"Don't you dare draw on him or attack him!" Melody flared.

"Draw? Attack?" For years North had dreamed of her coming out to his ranch, dreamed of her wanting him in her bed. Now she had done just that, but damn it, she was second-guessing everything he did in front of his men, especially Jeff, and Maria. "I'm not attacking anybody—yet."

"I know that superior tone of voice. You've used it enough times on me."

W.T. was watching him, watching her, listening to every order she dished out, his young face slack-jawed with amazement.

"Apparently not nearly enough," North growled.

"He wasn't doing anything wrong," Melody persisted.

"He's trespassing. But that's between him and me." He lowered his voice. "If you disagree, darlin', tell me so in private. Not here!"

"Oh, so nobody speaks up to the king in public?" Melody whispered back.

"This could be a dangerous situation."

"Come off your high horse, Rancher Black."

"Bienvenidos," Melody said aloud running up to the mysterious stranger. Her voice and actions were so defiant North wanted to shake her. "Welcome," she repeated sassily in English for all to hear.

Although the rider smiled down at Melody in an affable manner, his expression darkened dangerously whenever he looked at North.

North grabbed her arm and pulled her close, again lowering his voice to an undertone. "Do you have to act so thrilled by this man? He could be anybody—a smuggler, any sort of criminal."

"Don't be ridiculous."

"Tu mujer?" the man demanded with that flashy smile North found too familiar. *Your woman?*

"You're on El Dorado, my ranch." North stared at Melody.

"No." Melody eyed North and the stranger and then chirped tartly. *"Amiga."*

"For the last time, stay out of this, Melody." North sucked in a tight breath.

"I think he's cute and sweet," she whispered. "Maybe El Dorado has possibilities after all."

"He could be dangerous."

"You say that to inflate your...er...own position."

"Go inside—now."

"I can take care of myself."

"Like you did in the barn when you threw yourself in my arms?"

When she didn't budge, North was tempted to sling her over his shoulder and carry her to the house as he'd carried her out of Shorty's. Fortunately the stranger interrupted him in the middle of this furious train of thought with a tone of deep courtesy and abject apology.

"I do not mean to cause trouble. I'm afraid I seeked for water for my horse on your land when I saw the black birds circling. And I find *him*—little Teo in the brush. Very thirsty. Many days. Desert. No water." The dusty stranger glanced affectionately down at the boy in his arms. "He is a fighter."

"Teo?" North quizzed, really seeing the child for the first time. "You two together? *Familia?*"

"*No somos familia.* Teo and I, we camp in a hunting hut. Two days. I feed him there. Give him water." The rider patted a gourd strapped to his saddle. "From your well. I shoot strange pig. Feed him."

Melody gasped and studied the boy. Her eyes shining, she looked up at the man. "Oh, you were so wonderful. You saved his life."

"The kid's wet, Melody. So's your knight in dusty buckskin," North exclaimed, a little ashamed that his voice had a nasty edge. "Illegals."

"No, the boy's poor and desperate. But because of this wonderful man, he's still alive." Melody breathed in deeply, joy lighting her beautiful face as she regarded the boy's beaming savior and then North.

The stranger's admiring green eyes were glued on Melody. Jealousy and pity mixed in North as she stared at the thin little boy in rags in the interloper's arms with more affection than she ever seemed to feel for him.

Kids were supposed to be cute. Not skinny with an overlarge, round dirty head topped with long and irregularly cut black hair like this one. They shouldn't smell bad nor wear rags, either. They shouldn't cower and hold such wincing pain in their big, dark eyes.

"Delfino must've missed this pair when he made his little raid. Call him, Gentry."

Curious, North stared at the man's canvas sandals and at

the strange spurs buckled to his bare ankles. His multilayered saddle topped with a thick sheepskin fleece was no ordinary Mexican saddle.

"Where are you from?" North murmured, automatically slipping back into Spanish.

"Argentina," the man answered, in a lilting, educated accent. "*Gaucho.*" Jeff slipped his cell phone out of his hip pocket and punched in numbers.

The stranger was tall, golden and slim. He had friendly green eyes and teeth as white as Chiclets. Despite an outer layer of grime, he held himself erect with the unconscious air of an aristocrat. His black horse, for all that it was dirty and thirsty, too, was as noble as his master. In perfect control of this splendid mount, the man gently handed the limp little boy down to North.

"A good bed and a few good meals—he be fine," the stranger said.

"You're a long way from home," North replied, taking the child, whose bony frame was as light as air.

"I made a foolish bet, *señor.*"

The stranger threw a long leg over his saddle. In a single fluid motion the gaucho flung himself to the ground, landing beside Melody as gracefully as a dancer.

Acid churned in North's stomach when the handsome fellow tilted the brim of his dusty hat and smiled down at her. "Hugo Avila. At your service, mees."

"Melody Woods." She actually curtsied. "At yours."

Avila extended a lean brown hand, which she took. She would barely speak to North, but she fell all over this filthy stranger with pretentious airs.

"Call me Manolete...after the famous Spanish bullfighter."

"You must be very brave."

North swallowed hard. "You've never seen a bullfight in your life."

"Do you have to be so rude to him? He is your guest. He saved this child."

"My guest?"

"You two must be deeply in love," Manolete whispered way too knowingly.

"What?" North and Melody both erupted.

"The way you fight. The sparks they shoot, like how you say—fireworks. She looks so pretty, so passionate when she is *furiosa, enojada* with you, *señor.* If she is not your *mujer,* make her so—*muy rapido.*"

A screen door banged. When Sissy came running toward them, Manolete dropped Melody's hand and seemed suddenly transfixed.

"Tu mujer?" Manolete asked.

"My sister."

"Is she married?"

"What are you doing on my ranch? Who is this child?" North nodded at the boy in his arms.

"And who are you, *señor?"* Avila demanded with equal arrogance. "Where am I? I asked you a question. Is your beautiful sister married?"

"Why don't you ask her?"

Manolete couldn't seem to quit staring at Sissy's fine-boned face, dark hair or trim figure. When she joined them, he repeated his courteous bow. Manolete lifted her hand and kissed two fingertips. When he reached for the third, Sissy burst into giggles.

"What's with you?" Sissy demanded.

"Hugo Avila. At your service."

"King, I've got Delfino." Jeff shoved the cell phone into North's hand.

"Delfino?" Melody whispered as the boy's black lashes fluttered open.

"Teo," Melody whispered, "you are safe."

The child stretched out a thin dark hand with dirt-encrusted fingernails and bloody scratches. "Angelita—" The ragged child pressed a tiny piece of paper into her hand.

She lifted her gaze to North. "Who's on the phone?"

"Border Patrol."

"No!" Melody cried.

North covered the mouthpiece of the telephone with his palm. "Go inside and stay out of this, Melody."

"He just gave me a phone number with a Houston area code—"

"This isn't your fight."

"Fight? Does that darling child in your arms look like he's fighting?"

The kid's thin, dark face, his huge fearful eyes pierced North through the throat like the shaft of an arrow. "Down here, it's us against them," North said.

"This kid in your arms isn't a threat to you. But if you tell the Border Patrol about him, what will happen to him? He's what, twelve, at the most? He's all alone. No mother. No father. No country. He gave me a phone number. He's got family in Houston."

He stared at her.

"If it's a good idea to rat to Delfino now," she persisted, "why wouldn't it work to tell him later?"

"There's no way I can explain—"

"So, don't—" She grabbed the phone and punched End.

His men, Maria, the green-eyed stranger, and even the pitiful little boy he held, and no telling who else, were all watching them.

"What are you trying to do here, Melody? You come down here, then you use this kid to push me around in front of my men— Where do you see this going? You want to stick around for good? Hash out a lasting compromise on some very serious issues?"

"Y-you're taking this too far."

"Am I? I was the first. I can't seem to forget that."

Her beautiful voice softened. "This isn't about us. This child's life is in your hands."

The little boy in his arms began to tremble the way Little Camel did sometimes. She loved children. She wanted to

save this child, and as he looked into her beautiful blue
eyes, he wanted—

The hell he did. He stared at the child and then at her.
He eyed his men and Maria who were watching.

"All right. He can stay," North said. "For one night.
But only if you stay, too—to take care of him."

"What?"

Maria looked hurt. Jeff's mouth was agape. W.T. looked
slack-jawed. North could feel them all grappling to understand him even as he was.

"Give him to me," Melody whispered.

When Melody had the child, Teo smiled. North felt a
stab of remorse as he stalked toward Maria and let her slide
her arm around him.

"I can't believe you did that," Maria said.

"You want to know something. Neither the hell can I."

"He could be a thief from that bad *ejido*. Or worse, what
if he's a drug smuggler or works for the Midnight Bandit?
Whatever he is, he's illegal."

"Try telling her that."

"You did it for *her*."

And for a skinny, injured kid. "Can we talk about something else, Maria?"

"When is *she* leaving?"

"Tomorrow. First thing."

"*She's* spending the night? Oh, North, you can't be serious. She made a fool of you."

Dozens of times. "It's only one night, okay? The kid
needs a bed, care...."

In Maria's soft, understanding black eyes, North saw all
his own doubts about the evening ahead of them magnified
ten times over.

Nine

The night, his date with the perfect Maria, had barely gotten started, and already North was in one lousy mood. Maria, the rich ranch girl who understood him, wanted him to romance her, which a sane man with a lick of common sense would want to do.

Here he was hiding out in the kitchen with Jeff, rustling through the liquor cabinet.

She was upstairs, for the first time since forever. Melody hadn't taken his calls after that night in his apartment.

But Jeff hadn't taken hers, either, when she'd finally gotten up the nerve to talk to him. How many times had she tried to call him? She'd driven all the way out here to tell him she'd stayed up all night afterward. So had he.

Why the hell couldn't he stop thinking about it?

All of a sudden their argument over the illegals, the way she'd stood up to him in front of his men, didn't bother him nearly as much as it should have. He was too damn glad she'd finally come back to him. And that's what she'd done. Just as he'd said she would.

He was losing control.

Every time he looked at Maria, he saw Melody instead. He kept remembering Melody's mouth that night, the way she'd crawled all over him and then kissed him as if she was an expert until he'd exploded. He kept remembering how shy and surprised and adorable she'd looked. He was touched by her kindness to the kid, too.

He wanted Maria gone. He wanted Melody here.

He wanted to carry Melody to bed and make love to her. He didn't give a damn what Jeff or Gran or anybody else thought about it, either. It seemed to him that for as long as he could remember, he'd been on his own out here, with the ranch to manage and too many people to look out for, and too many people figuring out his life for him.

Now the woman he'd wanted for most of his life was here, and even though she always seemed hell-bent on making a fool of him, the burden and the loneliness of the ranch didn't feel nearly as heavy as usual. It was crazy. Maybe *he* was crazy. But always, *always* when she was around, he felt alive.

So, how to explain to Maria?

"Forget *her*," Jeff whispered behind him. "You know you said yourself that was the smart thing to do."

"Right." Easier said than done. Especially with him thinking maybe smart wasn't so smart after all.

What bedroom would Melody be in tonight? The one across the hall from his own? Or the one next to his with the door that didn't quite latch, the one that had the connecting balcony, too.

"How many times did Mel call the ranch?"

"Forget her."

North set the wine bottle down hard and glared at him. "Seven!"

Silently North reached across Gran's tattered deck of

cards on the kitchen table for an unopened bottle of Chardonnay.

"Maria said she wanted Merlot."

Melody's wine of preference was Chardonnay.

"Right. Merlot."

"So, open that one for her, why don't you," Jeff grumbled, shoving a bottle with the correct label toward North.

"Me, I prefer straight whiskey," North said to cover his blunder. Grabbing a bottle of whiskey from the cupboard that had a shot or two left, he opened the bottle and drained it in a gulp or two. Then he flung the bottle toward the trash.

He missed. The bottle rolled.

"Why didn't you get rid of *her* when you had the chance? If you aren't careful, she'll be leading you around by the nose again."

"She'll be gone soon enough."

"Will she? I have a mighty funny feeling."

North had more than a feeling. Maybe that's why he clamped his lips together and stared at the window at the barn for a long moment, and all the time he was listening for her light footsteps upstairs or for her impertinent voice calling to him.

She didn't belong here...with him.

What if she did?

"Why don't you concentrate on what's right about to-night—the good music, two beautiful women waiting for us in the den—easy women—and great steaks. The moon's gonna be big and bright, just off full, too. Not to mention wine and whiskey."

Jeff forgot his doubts. "We'll get 'em lit, get ourselves lit, take 'em out to a hunting cabin. The night's gonna be perfect."

Something made of glass exploded upstairs.

North cocked his dark head upward. "What the hell was that?"

"Her."

"She's in Daddy's room. Nobody's supposed to ever stay in that room."

"She's bound and determined to ruin our evenin' with Tina and Maria. Don't you dare go up and see—"

But North had slammed the Merlot bottle down and was already dashing from the kitchen through the den past Maria. When she rushed toward him, her pretty face worried, he quickly shook her off and bounded up the stairs two at a time.

When he flung his father's huge, antique Mexican door open and stormed through the sitting room to the bedroom, everybody froze. Sissy was on her knees before the sofa sweeping jagged bits of silver from the wooden planking. Apparently the ancient mirror his father had brought from Spain as a bridal gift to his mother had fallen off the wall.

North saw his dark face and Melody's paler defiant one when she joined him in the sitting room reflected in those gleaming shards.

"This isn't a guest room," North said. "Pick any other bedroom."

Melody had pulled back the sheets of his father's bed, so Manolete could put Teo there, but the boy was staring at the magnificent room, his big black eyes wide-eyed with wonder. When he saw North, his frail face tightened.

Pity pierced North's heart. "Don't you dare lay him there," North grumbled. "Get out of here. All of you. And you, Melody, I want you gone."

"Really," she said a little too brightly. "You did order me to stay. Am I right?"

"I wasn't in my right mind."

"Are we ever, when we're together?"

"Melody—"

"As you can see, I'm very busy."

"We don't use this room."

"Then it's time you did."

He stared at her.

"Why aren't you downstairs entertaining your beautiful,

perfect girlfriend?'' Melody queried, not in the least deterred by his temper or thunderous commands.

''Girlfriend?'' He drew a blank.

''Maria!'' Melody smiled. ''She's perfect, you know.''

''And dazzling,'' he agreed.

''So, why aren't you down there having fun with her?''

''Good question. Perfectly logical.''

She smiled up at him. She'd probably lifted the mirror from the wall and smashed it to the floor to get him up here.

He made a low animal sound. ''I heard you up here! He can't stay here!''

''Teo? Why on earth not?''

''Like I said, this is my father's suite.''

''I know.'' She directed her voice toward the bedroom. ''Manolete, lay him down on the bed and go.''

''I said no!'' North repeated.

The boy groaned.

An odd pang tugged in North's chest.

''Gently. *Cuidado,* Mano.'' Her voice was soft, imploring.

''Mano? Already you have a nickname for this stranger?''

''Don't be so jealous. Everyone calls him that,'' Sissy said, casting an affectionate glance toward Hugo.

''Jealous?'' North demanded. ''Who's jealous!''

''If the green boot fits, my darling—'' This from Melody.

She'd called him *darling*.

Since she had his full attention, Melody ignored him and turned to his sister. ''Sissy, take Manolete…leave us, please. I think your darling brother wants to be alone with me.''

''Damn it, that's the last thing I want!''

When they rushed to obey her, Melody pulled the bedroom door shut, and he found himself alone with her in his father's vast sitting room and feeling very uncomfortable.

"Who are you to give orders? In my house? When I told you Teo couldn't stay in—"

Melody moved toward him, and quite imperiously he thought. "Your father is dead, isn't he? Do you think his spirit is still here or something?"

"Have you no respect?"

"Maybe I do...for the living." Her voice softened dangerously. "For you."

"That's bull—"

"Well, if your daddy's spirit really is here," Melody began, "I'm sure he could do with a little company. After all Sissy says your mom's in Europe with a new lover—"

A chill went through him. "Don't you dare—"

"If I were your daddy, I certainly wouldn't want to be entombed for years and years in a musty smelling old room like this when everybody else was out having fun. I think your mother's lucky to be in love."

"How would you know?"

"How do you think? The way I felt...when you were with Claire...bleak and horrible. And then when you carried me out of Shorty's like you'd die if you couldn't have me..."

"That's over."

"Is it?"

Her smoky eyes glittered with a heat so wild and bright it threatened to consume him. He felt a strange pull from her, a mad desire to take her in his arms, to forget everything except her.

"When I kissed you like that...the other night," she said, "I—I never felt like that before."

Neither the hell had he.

Unconsciously she sucked in her lower lip, and a sudden shudder shook him. "You said I came back for more.... What if I did? What if I can't leave you alone? Even when you get impossible like you did with Mano and Teo? Even when you come up here and order us around like a great big bully?"

"I'm not a bully!"

"You can be sweet and cute and wonderful…sometimes. Even sensitive and big-hearted. After all, you let Teo stay." She hesitated. "You let me stay."

"I'm in no mood for your teasing."

"I'm not teasing."

A moment passed. He took a step toward her.

She whirled out of his reach and yanked a cord and the dark drapes swished open, flooding the room with reddish-gold light and a view of Gran's emerald-green front lawn stretching from the house to meet buff-colored desert.

"Oh, how beautiful your ranch is!" she exclaimed as if to change the subject. "When he's better, he'll be able to see Libby's jimsonweed and oleander right beneath this window. I'll tell him how the white blossoms close every night and in the heat of the day."

"He won't be here that long. Neither will you."

"I'm not the only one with hang-ups, now am I? Maybe I'm afraid of sex. But what are you afraid of, big guy?"

"Not a damn thing."

But when she came toward him with that gleam in her eye to know more, he backed against the wall as if he were a coward.

"You've been drinking. For courage? The same as I had to that night? Because you're scared of ghosts? Or scared of me? Or maybe both?"

She stopped within inches of him, so close he could feel the heat of her sweet young body. He swallowed, tasted whiskey and longed for more.

She forced her gaze up to his. "Why do you work so hard, North? Why do you have to be in charge of everybody and everything? Of me? Why do you have to protect? To rule? Why can't you ever just be? Just let me be? What is it with you, North? What makes you so uptight?" She stared around the room, her voice dying. "When I was in the barn, I remembered how your daddy died."

The light was going out of the day. Shadows enveloped the room. He couldn't think with her so near.

"You come out here," he rasped. "You think you know all the answers. You think you can run me and this place.... Because...because you look so damned pretty in that pink, and I have a weakness where you're concerned."

"A big one?" she murmured.

"Well, you can't order me around. We're finished."

"Are we?"

"You'd better call that number the kid gave you—fast. Because in the morning—"

"You shouldn't work so hard, North. You're killing yourself. Just like your daddy did."

"He didn't..."

In the fading light, in that pink outfit, she could have been standing there nude. She ran her hands up and down her slender arms, causing the little silver moons in her fingernails to flicker.

His heart began to pound violently as he stood statue-still, just looking at her.

"What do you want, North? I mean just for yourself? When you're not so determined to prove yourself worthy to your dead daddy?"

Desperately he swallowed. "Don't talk about him."

"You know what I think?" She laughed and then dived straight into his arms, like a child, sure of her welcome. "I think you want me. I think you want your own life! Same as I do. Only we're both too afraid...."

She looped her hands around his thick, muscular neck and reached up onto her tiptoes and kissed him. Her kiss was soft and a little clumsy, but wet and bold, too. The velvet early evening shimmered all around her, and soon he was gripping her to him so fiercely, her feet left the ground, and she gasped with pleasure.

"And I am afraid, North, just like you are."

When her tongue came inside his mouth and timidly explored, he shuddered at her exquisite and yet passionate innocence.

"What if we faced our ghosts together?" she asked.

Finally he managed to let her go. In a thick, barely controlled voice, he said, "I want you and this boy gone come morning."

"This is about your father isn't it? Your whole life is about him?"

"Stop."

"I crossed a line when I mentioned him? When I came in here? Sissy said you loved him very much. You did, didn't you?"

Pain and loneliness and grief consumed him. She saw it, and her eyes filled with tears.

"I don't want to cause you pain," she whispered, reaching a hand toward him.

He didn't want her pity.

"You want the truth? Is that what you want? I'll give you truth. I destroyed him! That's why he haunts me. I destroyed the finest man that ever lived! He was a hero. Everybody loved him. You wanted the truth— If I kill myself working, I'll never be a tenth as good as he—"

"North, I—"

"I have no right to set foot in this room and neither do you. And neither does that filthy kid you had the audacity to put in his bed!"

She went white, as if he'd hit her.

Sudden tears filled her eyes. "He's a precious human being. And so are you. He needs a doctor...."

North winced. "Like I said," he whispered, his voice as raw as his heart, "the sooner you leave, the better."

Quick hot tears spilled down her cheeks. But she didn't speak or cry out. Instead she rushed blindly past him and slammed out of the suite into the dark hall.

As he listened to her flying footsteps growing ever softer on the stairs, he sank down onto his daddy's sofa, the whiskey burning his gut.

The kid made some soft raspy sound.

North picked up the phone and called his doctor, who was a close personal friend.

"I have a big favor..."

Ten

Melody held the phone to her ear and listened as it rang endlessly. The doctor had come and gone, saying Teo needed rest and would be fine. "Come on! Answer the phone, whoever you are! A little boy's future depends on it!"

Melody's pulse throbbed. Her heart ached from her fight with North.

Too bruised to face him or the others anytime soon, she hid in the deep shadows of North's state-of-the-art, downstairs office across from the den. Frantically, for what had to be the tenth time, she punched in the numbers of the Houston phone number Teo had slipped into her hand.

"*Tiá* Irma," he had said as she'd told him good-night. *Aunt Irma.*

As Aunt Irma's phone rang again and again, Melody began to quiver like an overly sensitive antenna when she heard North's deeply melodious voice and Maria's an-

swering laughter from the den. How easily he'd gone from
her to Maria.

Feeling stupid and shattered, Melody gazed at the me-
diocre landscapes of ranch scenes on one wall, then at the
stern, black-and-white photographs of his ancestors on the
opposite wall. Her eyes fell to his computer, his laser
printer and then to his in-basket stacked with dozens of
neatly organized bills. When North's voice and Maria's
laughter seemed to grow louder, Melody thumbed nervously through his bills, realizing for the first time how
much he spent on utilities, tractor tires, bovine antibiotics,
irrigation systems and bulls. And those were only the first
six or seven bills. Why, just one tractor tire cost a thousand
dollars.

North lived such an adult life compared to her. She was
still in school, graduate school albeit, but still a child in so
many ways, not knowing how to be a woman in his bed
and at the same time stuck wondering what to do with the
rest of her life.

North didn't have the luxury of wondering. He had the
very real burden of running this immense ranch on his
shoulders, on his alone, with no one to help him, to stand
by him. Everyone at El Dorado looked to him to take care
of them. He really did need a wife, a mature woman ready
to support him, at least emotionally, a woman who understood his world, a woman like Maria.

On the twelfth ring Melody hung up in utter despair to
more of Maria's throaty laughter.

North had told Melody he couldn't wait for her to go.

How happy he seemed to be with Maria now.

Quietly, swiftly, Melody slipped out of the silent office
and raced back upstairs. To check on Teo, she told herself.

The scent of mesquite, baking potatoes and meat burning
drifted upstairs and soon made Melody's hunger win out
over heartbreak, causing her to decide to brave going downstairs and joining the others again.

Not that anybody seemed to notice her when she entered

the kitchen where dinner preparations were well under way. The table was set. Mano was whispering to Sissy in a dark corner while Libby was enjoying a game of solitaire at one end of the huge table while she drank her whiskey straight from the bottle.

North and Maria were outside with Jeff and Tina grilling steaks over an enormous mesquite bonfire. Watching North with his friends from the window above the sink made Melody feel even more than a fifth wheel as she glumly poured herself a glass of Chardonnay.

Since Mano and Sissy seemed so preoccupied with each other, she slipped onto the side screened porch. Sitting in a rocker behind hanging baskets of ivy and ferns, she was hidden from everybody and could enjoy the smell of the fire as she sipped her Chardonnay.

She'd forgotten to close the door. The warm evening breeze carried snippets of conversation from both the kitchen and the terrace.

North and Jeff were thrilling their dates with talk of their adventures with the Midnight Bandit, whoever he was.

"I knew there would be trouble when that Mexican on the other side of the Rio Grande sold his small rancho for at least four times the going price. Then the new owner trucked in all those expensive racehorses, brood mares with good bloodlines and prize stud horses, too. I never saw anyone legitimate in the horse business who could afford to spend money that fast.

"That doesn't make him the Midnight Bandit," Maria said.

"He wasn't there a week before somebody cut our fence and ran a thousand head of our cattle across the river to his place and then demanded ransom," Jeff said. "He set soldiers to guard our herd. North told me to go down there and bring them out, come hell or high water."

"Weren't you afraid of breaking international laws?" Maria asked.

"Not when I was knee-deep in the Rio Grande and I

almost got my horse shot out from under me. I was too damn scared to worry about anything but getting out of that jam alive.''

North looked grim, but he didn't say anything to verify Jeff's incredible story, and Melody couldn't believe it was true. Maria, however seemed to take the story as gospel.

How beautiful she looked, her olive face aglow in the firelight as she looked at North. How beautiful they looked together.

All of a sudden the Chardonnay had Melody's mouth feeling dry and cottony. Setting her empty glass on the wicker table beside her rocker, she curled her feet up under her. She felt left out and lonely as she used to around her own family when everybody was talking to each other and not her.

Her mother had wanted a beautiful daughter who wore makeup, beautiful clothes, a daughter like Claire, who followed the rules and married well. Her father had wanted a son.

But Melody felt even worse out here where she was a clumsy city girl and people expected North to marry a ranch princess...like Maria.

Was there no place Melody would ever belong? Was there no one she would ever belong to?

All her life she had tried so hard, too hard to be popular, to be loved, because deep down, she wasn't sure she was worthy of the kind of love she so desperately needed.

She shouldn't have driven out here.

North. North had always seemed so consumed by her, so addicted to her, so willing to put up with her in spite of her faults, so willing to wait for her to grow up. For years, she had taken his love for granted, even told him he was boring...because she'd been able to count on his predictable, steady, enduring, mature love.

Melody had wanted to be loved in that powerful way even if at the same time that sort of love had felt heavy and controlling and maybe even a little dull for someone of her supposedly free nature.

Maria was mature and beautiful—perfect for a mature man like North. She probably accepted that the bonds of love could limit a woman's freedom, limit her choices. She wanted North enough to make those necessary sacrifices.

Melody pressed her head against the back wall of the house. Life was so confusing. What did she want—really?

When she'd had North, she'd thrown him away. Now that she didn't have him, she felt as if she would die if she couldn't have him again. But if she got him back, would she just throw him away again? Was that fair?

She ran her hands through her hair. What was she doing here?

The group around the fire were speaking so low she couldn't hear them any longer. Now it was Mano's husky voice and Sissy's thrilled replies in the kitchen that held her attention.

"Argentina?" Sissy was saying. "How romantic!"

Mano's voice was husky. "This is more so. You are—"

North used to speak to her in that same sexy, desperate way.

"Don't say things you don't mean. I have been…unlucky in love."

"No more. To think, I would never have seen this pretty face if I had not drunk too much in a bar with my best friend."

"What do you mean?"

"We made crazy bets, he and I. I bet him I could travel from Argentina to New York City on horseback like my ancestor who was a French explorer. I read about him in family diaries. We both pledged that if I did it, we would give much money to the hospital where my father works as a doctor."

"How wonderful. So, what is Argentina like?"

"My father was born a rancher, so we have *estancia*. Very big even now. But the old days are gone forever."

"Here, too."

"Everywhere, *mi vida*."

"North tries so hard. Too hard—"

Why did he work so hard, so urgently? Why did that make her heart tug with a tight little pain?

"Did I tell you, you are very beautiful, Sissy."

"Too many times for me to believe you."

"When I reach New York and send for beautiful Sissy, will you believe me then?"

"We must wait and see what you say then and what I believe then."

"It is so exciting."

"What?"

"You. Me. Love. Like North and Melody."

Melody's breath caught when she heard their names.

"But he's dating Maria now," Sissy said.

"His heart belongs to Melody."

"Is our mysterious gaucho right? Is that really what's wrong with me?" a deep voice said in Melody's ear.

She whirled and then said nothing, her gaze widening as she beheld the blurrily familiar shape of a certain broad-shouldered individual framed by the pointy black leaves of the ivy that dripped from baskets on all sides of him.

"How long have you been out here all by yourself in the dark?" he whispered.

She felt dizzy, excited. "I didn't hear you come up."

"How's the kid?"

"Better by the hour."

He sucked in a deep breath. "I'm sorry," he said, curving his hand beneath her face as if she were infinitely precious.

Her heart had begun to beat in her throat. "Me, too."

"I didn't think." His thumb followed the smooth flesh of her shoulder. When she jumped a little, he hesitated. "I've had a lot on my mind."

"You were upset." He looked surprised when she tilted her head willingly toward his.

"I'm supposed to be with Maria tonight."

"She's beautiful, perfect—"

"All that and more," he agreed, his voice lazy. "And yet—"

"You said you wanted me gone upstairs."

"Yes. But why? That is the question."

There was a strange note in his deep voice that lit her heart. Melody waited, holding her breath.

"I want you gone—because you disturb me." His hand moved through her hair. "Because you can make me more miserable than anyone alive," he whispered, his voice hushed, tender.

"I know the feeling."

He broke away. "But then again—you make me happier."

"What are you saying?"

"I don't know." His free hand closed on hers and pulled it behind her waist, locking it there. Then he lowered his lips to the top of her head. "Everything, I suppose. You make me crazy. We quarrel." His lips were hot against her brow. "Then Maria flatters me when I most need flattering. She is so easy to be with, and yet all I can think of is what we started in my father's bedroom. Of what we started in my apartment."

Suddenly his soft, warm kisses against her forehead weren't enough. Nothing they'd ever shared was enough. She wanted his whole mouth. His whole body. His entire being. Everything—even though the thought of such total surrender terrified her.

She slid her hand instinctively along the white cotton material of his shirt and then lower, down the hard muscles of his thigh. "Oh, North— Me, too."

"Melody, I can't forget how it felt…being in your mouth."

Neither could she.

He whirled her around, so that she faced him. "Why did you do that?"

"I—I don't know. It just happened. I was afraid you would think I was terrible."

"Oh, darlin'—" His lips hovered near hers. For a breathless second she waited for him to kiss her hard.

She pursed her lips expectantly, aware of the elemental chemistry charging the air that separated her mouth from his. With an abandon that amazed her she stood up on her tiptoes and took the initiative.

Her lips met his. The kiss she began was soft, hungry, sweet, but cut short too soon.

"Supper," Jeff yelled right before he barged inside the screened porch with the platter of steaks along with Maria and Tina.

North cursed low under his breath as Melody jumped free.

All through dinner, Maria sat by North and flirted outrageously with him. Jeff pretended that the romantic night he'd set up was going just as he'd intended, that Melody's presence made no difference.

Melody felt North's edgy tension every time his brooding gaze fell on her. What had the near kiss meant to him? Was he as consumed by her as she was by him? Or did he see it as a mistake now?

Maria and he talked ranch stuff. Then the conversation turned to the growing problems they had with illegals. Everybody tried to explain to Mano why they'd been so alarmed when he'd ridden up.

"—They come on our ranches—"

"It's different now. Two weeks ago three of them held the ranch manager at *Rancho Tigre* at gunpoint."

"But Mano is on a mission," Melody said. "And Teo's just a child. How do you know they aren't all—"

Maria was shaking her head, looking at North, sure he'd agree with her.

"Melody has a valid point," North said, his eyes kind as he conceded to her. "We shouldn't mistreat children. There's no excuse—ever."

"Pass the potatoes," Libby said, as if she'd decided that paying more attention to his change of tact wasn't such a good idea.

There were eight people around the kitchen table, and all Melody wanted was to be alone with North again. Why had he taken her side in front of them? Did he feel the same as she—that tonight, if only they found their chance, she and he could bridge the chasm that separated them and make their own safe, cozy little world?

Manolete began to talk about his passion for bullfighting. When Melody got so interested, she began asking him questions, North began to scowl hard from his end of the table.

"I used to fight bulls, too—when I was a kid," North interjected.

"I can't believe that," Melody said with a smile. "You're no daredevil."

North looked at her with an intensity that scared her.

"Oh, but he was," Sissy said, "before Daddy died."

A look passed between brother and sister.

"What does she mean, North?" Melody asked.

"Not a damned thing," he said.

Startled by his harsh, impassioned voice, Maria and Tina turned to stare at him at the same time.

"North used to be wild...impulsive. Everybody said so," Sissy persisted.

"Shut up—" North's face had darkened. His eyes glittered. Slowly, as if he held himself under a tight leash, he got up from the table and poured himself another whiskey. Slamming the cabinet doors, he came back to the table and sat down. "I grew up. I got some sense. It happens to everybody."

"So, how's the kid doing?" Maria asked Melody in a cool, stilted tone, as if she also had decided this topic of conversation was too charged.

"He's okay. He went straight to sleep. I tried to call his aunt."

"And?" Maria queried.

"No answer."

"He ain't got no aunt in Houston," Jeff said matter-of-factly between large mouthfuls of steak.

"How long are you going to let the kid stay here, North?" Maria asked, shaking her head.

Melody's gaze flew to North when the kitchen went ominously silent. Without so much as a glance her way, he shoved his chair back, flung the screen door open, and then stomped outside, scraped his scraps on the ground with a knife and whistled for his dogs.

The screen door banged. When everybody looked at her, especially Jeff, Melody pressed steepled fingers to her mouth. It was a defensive gesture. Jeff blamed her for ruining tonight, for ruining far more than tonight.

"The Border Patrol has fought a lot of battles for us, let me tell you, city girl," Jeff said, a bitter note in his voice. "A lot of illegals are dangerous. We've gotta be careful...and fair. You've put him in a hard place." He hesitated. "But then that's always been your specialty."

Melody's chest tightened. When they, especially Maria, continued to glare at her, she felt heat in her cheeks. But before she could say anything to defend herself, the phone rang.

Jeff grabbed it. Almost instantly, his red eyebrows came together and his ruddy face turned purple.

"The Midnight Bandit?" Jeff exploded from his chair. "He what?" After another minute or two Jeff put a broad freckled hand over the mouthpiece and yelled toward the back door. "Hey, King, W.T. says Arturo called. Says there's a big new hole in our new fence down at La Negra. Signs of heavy trucks—"

North, who was still outside, didn't answer.

"Do you really think it's—the Midnight Bandit?" Maria asked.

Jeff's eyes were like ice. He slammed the phone down.

"So, what's with this Midnight Bandit?" Melody whispered tightly as North pushed the door open and stepped back inside. "Is he a joke or what?"

"You think he's a joke? You would, city girl," Jeff snapped.

"The name alone," Melody said lamely.

Jeff gave her another hard-eyed look. "Obviously we don't know his real name. W.T. made it up till we get a formal introduction in polite society."

"Oh."

"I have a hunch we're going out ridin' tonight, lookin' for him," Jeff said. "And pretty soon. Want to come, city girl?"

North bolted across the room and glared first at Melody and then at Jeff. "Don't you dare invite her on something like this, Gentry."

"Can I go, North?" Maria's voice had a wistful quality.

"Everybody but Melody," North snapped. "You can shoot straight."

"So can I," Melody volunteered.

"You've got the kid to see about, remember?" North said. "Teo needs you."

So, he thought Maria was more useful than she.

Manolete and Sissy decided to stay at the ranch, too.

"We better git," Jeff said, pouring his whiskey into a tall stainless steel mug and screwing the black lid on tightly.

Melody couldn't believe it when everybody sprang up from the table and went to the gun safe in the den and started grabbing shotguns and rifles. North was strapping his Colt revolver onto his hip and shouldering a shotgun. Jeff passed everybody rifles and shotguns and then poured three more stainless steel mugs full of whiskey.

"We'll be driving off road," Jeff explained. "This could be a long night."

"Are you crazy? This isn't the Wild West," Melody cried.

"You sure about that, city gal?" Jeff challenged as North grabbed a box of shells.

"North, you're acting as crazy and macho as Jeff. If you're really worried, why don't you call the Border Patrol?"

"We will—when it's time," North said.

"When it's time?" She stared at them, not understanding.

"You're the one harboring an illegal," Jeff said.

Everybody laughed at her.

Everybody but North.

"You're pathetic, North. And you're drunk, Jeff. You're living in a fantasy world. I don't believe there's any such thing as the Midnight Bandit."

"Then you're the one who's living in a fantasy world," Jeff hollered as he flew out the back door. "We want our cows, and we can't afford an international incident. We'll call the Border Patrol, when we've got the bandit and our cows—on this side of the border." He waited on the others. "Let's go."

North headed across the kitchen after Jeff.

Melody ran toward him, suddenly scared for him. "North, I can't believe you're—"

He slanted a look down at her. Then he walked out the door.

She waited, alone in the house. Outside the truck roared. When she got to the garage, the truck's red taillights were disappearing down a rutted road into the thick brush.

Then she was running, crying North's name until she was choking the clouds of dust billowing from the truck into the grass and weeds.

The truck didn't stop.

North was gone.

With Maria. After the Midnight Bandit. Or some such nonsense.

And she was all alone.

Slowly, wrapping her arms around herself, she mounted the stairs to check on Teo.

Eleven

Melody should have known better than to take a shower in such a big old ranch house in the middle of the night. North had been gone for hours. Her upstairs bedroom with its wall of windows along the upper balcony was bright and warm by day. It would have been cozy by night, if she'd drawn the drapes. But after she'd checked on Teo again she'd come inside and tried his aunt's number again.

Aunt Irma had answered. She'd sounded surprised at first and had said that she didn't own a car, but that she'd come as soon as she could arrange transportation. Melody had told Teo and then read for a while and left the drapes open. Now that she was in the shower and could relax about Teo, she was anything but relaxed as she realized there was a lot of dark glass, a lot of exposure at night.

One minute she was arching her body under the warm spray of the shower spigot, trying to rid herself of the inner chill in her soul North's desertion had caused. Spumes of delicious steam were curling all around her as she hummed haltingly and shampooed her hair with shaky fingers.

Then the hardwood floor beyond the bathroom creaked softly. Terrified, she remembered a twig that had cracked right before those boys had started chanting when she'd walked home.

When a drawer opened and closed, she dropped the bottle of shampoo with a clatter and hugged herself.

North had gone off to chase the Midnight Bandit. What if the rogue was for real? What if he was here? What if there was no one awake in the house but her?

She had locked the hall door, but had she checked all the balcony doors? Shrinking against the back wall, her overactive imagination did a replay of the shower scene in that old horror film, *Psycho*. She saw the killer's horrible shadow against the shower curtain, heard the screams.

Stop it, Melody. You aren't by yourself. Libby's probably still playing solitaire. Teo is just down the hall asleep. Manolete and Sissy are somewhere outside. There's no Midnight Bandit. And even if there was, he's down on the border cutting fences and driving heavy trucks around. She kept talking to herself as she stood under the showerhead to get the soap out of her hair.

A boot heel on wood brought her reassuring self-talk to a standstill. No sooner had she turned off the faucets—the better to hear the big bad wolf or whomever was out there—than the bathroom door creaked and a man's broad-shouldered shadow fell against the opposite wall.

"Who's there?" she squeaked, closing her eyes, not wanting to see.

"Just me," came North's deep undertone, causing her heart to knock against her rib cage with a new kind of excitement and a special kind of fear.

"I didn't mean to scare you," he said, his voice deliberately gentle. "I knocked. You didn't answer. I wanted to make sure you're okay."

She couldn't answer. Her shyness and fears warred cra-

zily with her desires as she opened the shower door and
stepped blindly into the mists, almost falling into his arms.
He ripped a towel off the rod and handed it to her.

"I looked in on Teo. He has more color. You're amaz-
ing." She couldn't stop staring at North. He was so beautiful, heart-stoppingly gorgeous. His damp black hair waved
silkily across his forehead; his black eyes were fierce with
an emotion every bit as strong as whatever she felt.

"Did you catch your bandit?"

He shook his head. "I kept thinking about you back here
all alone. So, I left Jeff to do the dirty work."

She smiled impishly, ignoring the towel in his hand.
"Why did you come back?"

"I think you know," he murmured.

"What about Maria?"

"I told her how I felt about you."

Melody studied him. "You did, huh?" She laughed. Instead of taking the towel from his large, brown hand, she
continued to tease him breathily. "Then don't just stand
there. Dry me off."

"I'm the king but you're giving the orders. Not that I'm
objecting."

She was naked, timidly so, but trembling with longing.
He was fully dressed in his old jeans and white work shirt,
his long sleeves rolled up to his elbows. How dark his
amber skin looked against the white material. He was wearing the Colt revolver on his right hip again as if he were
dead serious about that bandit.

When his eyes flared, she forgot the gun and the mysterious outlaw that kept him up at odd hours. The way he
looked at her made her feel bolder and more beautiful than
ever before—and desirable. Maybe she wasn't any good at
this, maybe she wouldn't ever be, but he'd left Maria, the
perfect lady, and come back to her anyway. Never had he
made her feel more precious than now as he slowly, carefully folded the towel around her.

"You are beautiful. Incredible," he whispered, causing her to glow as he dried her.

Enveloping her completely in the thick, fluffy cotton, he began to rub her down. She didn't resist his ministrations, not even when he slid the towel between her legs, not even when he wrapped it around her waist and used it to compel her into his arms.

The minute her body came into contact with his, more sweet, wild yearnings seared her even as new fears threatened to send her flying out of the room.

"Are you sure about this?" he whispered. "You don't have to. If there's any hope I'll wait."

She'd wanted to be with him, wanted this strange, terrifying sweetness, wanted to know the pleasure of his hard mouth against her flesh. She'd been so stricken when he'd left her. But always she was of two minds, and now that he was here, she wasn't so sure as she felt the fever heat of his skin. He was immense, uncompromisingly male, all too capable of overpowering her.

He wanted her.

Like those disreputable boys had wanted her.

Not like those boys.

North loved her.

And if she couldn't prove to him she was ready to be his woman, she might lose him to someone else who would, maybe even to Maria. It was now or never. Melody knew there came a moment, when one simply had to seize what one wanted regardless of the risk...or risk losing far more.

"You stay right here, cowboy," she murmured shudderingly. "Kiss me."

When he hesitated, she knew he was afraid of what she might do. So, she dropped the towel to the floor and threaded her fingertips through the dark whorls of hair beneath his molten throat. Then undoing several buttons, her fingertips traced ever lower until she made hardened nubs of his nipples.

He ripped off his shirt and removed his gun. Carefully

he laid holster and revolver on the tiled floor. Then he rose to his full height and pulled her against him again, mashing her breasts against his hot, bronzed torso.

"You came back," she whispered, beginning to burn for him even as she tingled with fear.

His lips touched her throat. "I kept thinking about what you started the other night. And about you being here...all alone. I thought if you had the nerve to try again, hell, so did I."

Her fingers caressed the ridges of his biceps in terror but in wonder as well. "North, I don't know what I'm doing anymore. I never seem to know. I'm not sure you can count on me. I want to be all grown up, a real woman—your woman. But...I want to be my own woman, too, and I'm not sure that's what you want."

He stood motionless as she stroked him, letting her take the lead as he had at his apartment. "One day at a time. If you give me tonight, we'll have that. If that's all we ever have, at least we'll still have that."

When her arms slid around his neck, she felt his body tense. In a way he was as scared as she was.

She lifted her lips to his. When he began to kiss her, his mouth was soon so hot and urgent she forgot to be brave and pulled shyly away.

"Scared?" he muttered thickly, letting her go.

She hugged him tighter, buried her face against his hot chest. "Even if I am, don't stop," she whispered against his throat. "Promise not to stop. See, I've got to get through it. I've got to."

She heard his harsh indrawing of breath. Then his hand stroked her wet hair. "But I want you to enjoy it. To enjoy me. It's not supposed to be an ordeal."

"I won't know what's on the other side till I get there."

He smiled a slow, warm, sexy smile. "Okay, I don't know the answers. I just want to be with you now, tonight. Maybe someday we'll figure the rest out—why you're scared, I mean, and what to do about it."

"Someday... Tonight, let's just follow your instincts."

He seemed disinclined to argue. Easily he picked her up and carried her to the bed. Then he kissed her there as if he were starving. His tongue came inside her mouth with a greedy passion that threatened to devour her. She returned his kiss with such fierce ardor that it was a long time before he let her go. When he did so, he was trembling just as she was.

Quickly he undressed. As she watched him, she felt his passion building, but when he was done, he took her into his arms and kissed her gently. And slowly, oh, so slowly, turned her to flame.

As his lips moved from her face, down her throat, to her breasts, she forgot her fears. He wasn't forcing her. He loved her. He hadn't said it, but she knew. He wanted her, not Maria. Not perfect Maria. He wanted her, even if she couldn't ever fit into his world. Even if she was lousy at sex.

Lousy or not, an odd sensation began to build, a mysterious pressure that began in her belly, a fierce expanding neediness, for what exactly she did not know. She just lay there beneath him, her heart aflutter, clinging to him, dissolving in him, sighing, waiting, not knowing what to do to pleasure him, only knowing that she seemed to be brimming over with new breathtaking needs, until suddenly she felt near bursting. Still, as he wooed her with controlled kisses, the feeling inside her built until she felt herself near some fatal ecstatic edge that both terrified and thrilled her.

"I want to taste you, too," he whispered.

She didn't understand until he lowered his black head, and kissed her ever so tenderly down there.

A moan escaped her lips, and then it struck her, really struck her where his mouth was, how embarrassing and unladylike what he was doing was, and she tried to squirm free. But he held her legs apart and kissed her until what he did felt too good to fight, so she lay still. And suddenly it seemed that what he was doing made her feel most ladylike, and she wrapped her arms around his head as a fierce wildness consumed her. And he kept kissing her and stroking her until she had to cover her mouth to keep from crying out as wave after lava wave of passion swept her and gave her some mysterious release she'd never dreamed possible. And in that moment, she felt complete, and she loved him as she'd never dreamed she could. No other adventure seemed as great as just being like this with him.

Only when he felt her go utterly limp and sigh did he let her go. Only when he'd reduced her to a puddle of sensual languor did he circle her with his arms and crush her to him.

"Put your legs around my waist," he ordered.

When she obeyed she felt him there, poised at the center of her being to plunge inside and possess her, poised to mate in the most primal way.

And she wanted him to, more than she'd ever wanted anything.

"For a girl who doesn't like sex, you're very hot," he whispered.

"For you. Only for you."

"I love you," he said.

"I love you, too."

"I've waited for you longer than I ever believed I could wait for any woman."

"I know."

"But it was worth it."

"I was good then?"

"Don't you know?" he whispered.

She beamed, feeling very proud and happy, and very, very special.

"Was I perfect?"

"We're not through," he whispered. "Not by a long shot."

All that mattered was that he'd waited for her, that he loved her and that she loved him.

He thrust into her with the hard urgency of a man who'd

denied his own needs far too long, and then he stilled, their bodies joined.

He was bathing her face with tender kisses when his cell phone rang.

She jumped.

"Shh. Maybe it'll quit," he whispered, staying inside her, holding her.

But it didn't.

"Damn," he growled in an almost painful breath against her hair.

The jarring, electronic beeping was growing louder and more insistent with every ring. Soon he was swearing in a hard, angry undertone and rolling off her.

"Lord." He covered his eyes with his hand and then reached for it.

Melody lay in the dark, her eyes closed, rubbing her temples, impassioned almost to a point of insensibility and yet feeling abandoned, rejected—incomplete somehow. "Who—"

"Jeff." North was pulling out his antenna, pressing Talk. "I promised him I'd leave it on."

"Jeff?"

"In case he ran into trouble—"

"You're going to talk to Jeff now?"

"I'm real sorry, darlin'."

Jeff didn't say much, but before long North was cursing again. Ripping the covers aside like a big angry bear, he jumped out of bed and then yelped when his toe struck something hard.

"Ouch!" He began hopping on one foot. "My God! Where—"

Startled, she sat up as he lumbered clumsily across the dark to her bathroom. Slamming the door, he bolted himself inside, so she couldn't hear the rest of their conversation.

She got up. Running after him, she beat frantically on the locked door. "North, what's going on?"

He didn't answer, so she put her ear to the door. He was in the shower. She could hear the water.

He was going. Leaving her.

Feeling cold with a strange terror and curiously let down, she crawled back into bed. When he strutted into the bedroom a few minutes later, his expression was stern, and he was wrapped in a towel. Wearily he finger-combed his wet black hair back into place.

"What is it?"

"Nothing."

"Nothing? You spring out of bed like a cannon went off, and it's nothing?"

"This isn't any of your business, Melody."

What was she—a grown-up woman he took to bed when it pleased him, but a child he was determined to protect when it came to his real life?

"If it's nothing, you'd better come back to bed and finish what you started."

He grinned, clueless as to the depth of her concern. "For a girl that didn't want to, you're mighty eager all of a sudden. A guy like me could get cocky."

"I want to be your woman—in all areas of your life."

"Darlin' there's nothing I'd like better than to come back to bed."

He tugged on his jeans.

"But you're getting dressed! Why are you leaving me?"

He pulled his shirt on and began to work clumsily at the buttons.

"You can't start this after all your years of badgering me and then quit right in the middle," she added.

He managed a grin. "You used to, darlin'. For years and years, remember? Now you know how it feels."

"That's not fair."

"Fair. I run out one night! For a damn good reason! You made it a habit for years!"

"Because I was scared! You're doing this for some stupid, macho reason!"

"Darlin', I'll be back. I swear. I wouldn't miss tonight with you for anything. You're everything! Everything, do you understand!"

"If I'm everything, take me with you!"

His expression darkened as he approached the bed. "No. I can't risk anything happening to you—not ever. Especially now that we've finally found each other. Understand?"

No, she didn't.

"This is dangerous, isn't it?"

He shook his head. But something dark and alarmed in his voice and eyes as he held her close and petted her hair scared her and told her not to argue, not to make him suspicious.

"Darlin', I know what it is to do something stupid and lose somebody. You've got to stay here, where it's safe. If you don't—" His black eyes were fierce, almost threatening.

"Are you going to be in danger?"

"Who me? Not me." He kissed her hard.

He was lying. She could feel it. But if he read her mind and realized she might do something impulsive, there was no telling what he might do to stop her. She could tell he was very determined. So, instead of accusing him, she smiled obediently.

When he was done with his kisses, she curved her lips sleepily. Languidly she yawned and pulled the covers up and pretended to close her eyes.

"Hurry back," she said. "I can't wait!"

"Neither can I."

Satisfied that she was the obedient child he wanted her to be and would do as he asked, he kissed her lips one final time, held her again as if she were infinitely precious to him and then stalked out of the room.

No sooner had he shut the door, than she threw back the sheets and flew to the bathroom. In the dark she stumbled

over something hard. She flicked on the light and saw he'd
forgotten his gun.

Jeff had been out chasing the Midnight Bandit when he'd
gotten into trouble. She knelt, panic welling inside her as
she picked it up.

Almost she thought of running with it to the door and
calling him back. Instead her hand slowly tightened on the
carved leather holster and let herself grow used to how
heavy and deadly it felt.

Revolvers were the easiest guns in the world to use. At
least her daddy always said so. A girl didn't have to be all
that mechanical to use one. That's why he'd taught Claire
and her how to shoot one. He'd taken them to the bay,
thrown cans out, and told them to shoot.

"That way when you miss, you see where the bullets hit
in the water, so you know how far your aim is off," Sam
had said.

After a miss or two, Melody sunk twelve cans in a row,
and he'd proclaimed her a natural talent.

"You're as good as a man, honey."

"Better," she'd replied.

Easing the black revolver out of the holster, Melody re-
leased the cylinder and spun it just to make sure it was
loaded.

It was.

Her eyes drifted along the row of extra bullets North had
jammed into the leather belt. For a minute longer she knelt
there on the bathroom floor, holding the gun—her whole
body was paralyzed, literally so scared at the thought of
what she intended to do, she couldn't move. Could she
shoot a man when all she'd ever practiced on were soda
pop cans?

Then she thought of North going out to face whatever
or whomever it was that had Jeff wild with fear and had
made North leave her bed at a time no man would ever
leave unless he had to—alone.

What if something terrible had happened to him just

when she realized how much he'd always meant to her as well as how much more he could grow to mean? What if he needed her out there?

Idly she played with the leather belt, her fingers fiddling with the extra bullets, moving them up and down in their leather loops. Why did men think they were the only ones who could be heroes? Would she be any more capable of forgiving herself if something happened to him than he would be if something were to happen to her?

She sprang up and got dressed even faster than he had.

He would be furious. Maybe furious enough to storm out of her life forever.

North saw male-female roles in black-and-white terms. He thought women should be sweet and modest and obedient and sexy. He had never approved of her impulsive, adventurous spirit. There were certain areas of his life, he considered a man's domain. But if she was to grow up, didn't she have to become brave and whole and modern in all areas of her life? Not just their bedroom? If she were his equal, she couldn't let him order her around like he was a king and she was a serf. Not tonight—when his life might be in danger.

If she was ever going to really be a woman, North's woman, she had to follow him, no matter what it cost her.

Thus, when he slipped out of the house into the dark, she was right behind him.

Twelve

It seemed to North that he and Timmy Star had been squatting in the plane on the runway for nearly an hour.

"Star, haven't you revved your damn engine long enough?"

North flexed his hands, fisting them and then flexing them time and again. Jeff could be dead by now.

He kept seeing Melody's blue eyes ablaze with desire as she'd lain beneath him. She'd wanted him. Finally. She'd actually reveled in it. More than anything, he had to get back to her—fast.

The gravelly roar of the engine betrayed the fact Star had tampered with the plane to increase its horsepower significantly.

"Hold your horses, Black! I don't wanna just git you into Mexico so you can settle your score with the Midnight Bandit. I wanna git myself back to the civilized world."

When the sound of the big engine suddenly changed,

Timmy almost purred, "The prop's feathered. Ready for takeoff?"

As they taxied down the dirt strip lit by crude kerosene lamps, known as *bombas* in Mexico, in the stripped down, single-engine plane, North cursed the rotten luck that had gotten him out of Melody's soft arms and warm bed on this fool's errand just when she'd finally decided sex might be fun. But at least she was home safe.

He glanced at Timmy. Star was bald and fat. His complexion was baby-pink; his teeth were bad. Except for the gray plastic handle of what looked like a very serious military weapon peeping out from under his seat, Tim didn't look or act like a hotshot pilot turned smuggler. He had a wife, kids and a mortgage. He went to church most Sundays. But in this dangerous business, he was known for nerve.

Star had flown jets in the Gulf War. When he'd gone broke during a peso devaluation, he'd bought an old plane and gutted it down to the bulkheads. Other than the two front seats, there was nothing on board that wasn't necessary to flight. Thus, the large cavity behind their seats could be filled with contraband clear to the tail. He'd smuggle anything but dope—people, weapons—but not dope. Dope was dirty.

North couldn't quit thinking of Melody. Most of all he couldn't quit remembering how good he'd felt inside her.

As soon as they were airborne, they swung to the south toward the shadowy glimmer of the Rio Grande.

"She feels heavier tonight," Tim bellowed over the engine and vibrations.

"What?"

"The plane. I can always tell. You sure all you brought was two shotguns?"

"Maybe you've put on a few pounds."

"Too many tacos?" Star patted his belly.

They laughed, but nervously.

North peered over his shoulder into the gloom. "Just my guns."

"The tail feels heavy."

"Relax."

Tim grunted.

"How come you do this? I mean—you've made enough to quit long ago," North asked.

"Adrenaline. It's a rush. After what I did in the military, watching sitcoms every night won't do it."

They were barely in the air ten minutes before Timmy cut the power and banked sharply to the left. They had to fly low to get under the radar. A minute later had them on a fast sliding descent into utter blackness.

"Better get the lights turned on down there, boys—"

Down. Down. They seemed to fall endlessly into a black hole. North leaned forward, his heart thudding like a drum in his ears as he peered out. Expecting trees to rip into the fuselage any second, he held his breath. Flying at night with no lights, ducking and diving over rough country, there was always the possibility that they were off course, that a set of power lines might loom up suddenly.

North breathed a sigh of relief when a ragged line of *bombas* flashed on, marking the ranch landing strip that seemed to be in the middle of nowhere.

Then they were on the potholed strip, bumping to a standstill. The runway lights were instantly snuffed. North grabbed his guns and waited for the prop to crank down.

North slapped two thousand dollars in cash into Tim's hand, grabbed his guns, kicked the door open and stepped onto the wing. "Thanks."

Star stuffed the cash into the back pocket of his jeans. "Flying into Mexico is nothing compared to what I used to do in the military."

"Okay, so, sit tight. If I'm not back in an hour—"

"You know the rules. Any sign of trouble, and I'm outta here."

"Gotcha."

North was about to jump to the ground when an all too familiar, feminine voice behind them said, "Wait for me, Bertie!"

"What the hell!" Tim had his gun aimed on their stowaway in the dark cavity faster than North could blink.

"Rough landing," Melody said cheerily. "Other than that, great flight!" She smiled at Timmy. "Don't shoot. I'm with Rancher Black."

"You didn't say nothin' about no woman. I ain't waiting, Black. Not if you take her! Won't baby-sit her, either!"

"We had a deal—"

"Yeah—deal was—I'm outta here at the first sign of trouble." He propped his big gun across his legs and stared at Melody. "And I know trouble when I set eyes on it. She's it with a capital *T*. She's the little hellion that did the dance at that bar?"

"How the hell am I supposed to get back if you go?" North growled.

"That's your problem! Fly out now! Or get!"

"I'll settle up with you later. Take her with you."

"No way," Star said.

Melody beamed.

North reached back into the cabin and seized Melody's wrist so hard, she whimpered.

"What did you think you were doing tonight, darlin'?"

"Adrenaline. Maybe I like the rush."

Star laughed. "You've got yourself a real little troublesome spitfire. You two have fun."

North was so enraged, he could have strangled them both, but he concentrated on Melody and yanked her out of the plane.

"You little fool. You could be jeopardizing everything. The bad guys who have Jeff and my cattle are about as friendly as a den of rattlers."

She whitened and had the good sense to lower her eyes. Then she said, "Sounds to me like you need reinforcements."

"Not you."

"You should have told me the truth then."

"Oh, so it's my fault you're here?"

That she blamed him for putting her in danger made him even angrier. "You put yourself in danger, understand? You put Gentry in danger, too."

He jumped from the wing to the ground and reached up for her.

"So what happened tonight? What's wrong?" she asked when she landed lightly beside him.

"After Gentry took Maria and Tina home, he saw somebody messing with the trucks he loaded this afternoon. He went over to see what was going on. The Midnight Bandit and his men got him and the trucks and drove them across a low water bridge into Mexico. They're going to demand a ransom of some sort. No telling where they'd be if one of my trucks hadn't hit a rock. They've stopped to change a tire. They left Gentry in the locked cab. They didn't realize he still had his cell phone."

A dog barked. Suddenly they heard the roar of heavy machinery.

"Big truck at the end of the runway," Tim yelled as he began to rev the plane. "You've got company."

"Notify the border patrol," North said.

As Star taxied down the runway, the truck's high beams caught North in their blinding glare.

North grabbed Melody's hand and took off running for the thick brush.

It was hard for Melody to keep up with North as they marched through the high, dry, prickly grasses.

Once she fell on the rocks and cut her hand. North wrapped his handkerchief around it and told her she wouldn't be in this jam if she'd done what he told her.

"I got scared—for you."

"That's bull. You just acted on impulse. Like you did when you ran down the aisle and left me standing in front of all those people. Like you did when you danced at Shorty's and got all those shrimpers in a frenzy. You never give a damn when you turn my life upside down! What if you get you or me killed...or Jeff?''

''I couldn't let you go alone,'' she whispered raggedly.

''Stay close to me, and don't say another word till we get home.'' He knotted the handkerchief. ''Just do exactly what I say. Understand? They could be anywhere. And not just them. The border's alive with wets, *coyotes* and all sorts of unsavory characters who prey on them.'' He paused. ''You little fool. If anything happens to you, I'll never forgive myself.''

''Ditto, you big macho lug,'' she said silently as she trudged after him.

''Do you have a plan? Or... Or we going to walk all night?'' she whispered.

''Keep quiet.''

''So, a woman isn't supposed to think? She's just supposed to take orders?''

''Is that so hard?''

''Impossible.''

He was cursing low under his breath when they heard a dozen men cock their rifles.

A line of soldiers stood straight in front of them.

''Levantese los manos.''

North grabbed her by the hair and shoved her down into the grasses. The beam of their flashlights struck North full in the face.

''Don't move!'' Then he used the same voice he had used in her bed—it was deep, intimate, urgent. ''Please—''

He began yelling at them in Spanish, and they yelled back. Slowly he raised his hands, held his guns high and walked toward them.

Several of the men fanned out into the pasture with spotlights. Melody pressed her head to the warm dirt, scared they would hear the violent thumping of her heart. When, at last they gave up their search and rejoined the others,

Melody peeped her head above the grasses and saw that North was completely surrounded by men in brown uniforms. They were laughing at him now. Even though it was well after midnight, they all sported mirrored, aviator glasses. A big man with a flashy gold watch seemed to be in charge.

For a long time she stayed where she was frozen against the ground by fear. Only when they stripped North of his guns, tied his hands behind his back, and marched him roughly away did she regain enough of her courage to get up and follow them.

They stopped and she hung back, so scared she bit her lips and then her tongue. So scared she hadn't realized she'd drawn blood until they were out of sight again and she tasted copper.

Dear God, what were they going to do to him?

She loved him. She'd never known how much until now. He had waited for her to grow up. He would lay down his life for her. He just had.

He'd gone against his friends and come back to the house tonight. He'd let Teo stay even though it was against the law and his deepest principles—for her. He'd called the doctor for Teo.

She loved him. She couldn't let him die.

They would kill him for sure—if she didn't do something—fast.

But what?

What could one scared girl do against so many?

In Mexico?

Thirteen

Cows mooed and shuffled heavily in the pair of cattle trucks the bandits had parked beside the narrow dirt road. Three Mexicans in uniforms and mirrored glasses were kneeling over a back wheel, running their palms along the heavy tread of the big tire they'd just changed.

Melody stared as one wiped his face with a bandanna. Then her gaze wandered to the others clumped around the fire. They'd butchered one of North's cows and were cooking meat over a spit. North and Jeff were bound and gagged in the cab of their own cattle truck filled with bawling cattle.

She closed her eyes. It seemed she'd stood in the dark here for hours, her heart numb with terror, her mind paralyzed by indecision.

One of the Mexicans opened the cab and started the engine. After he'd carefully backed the big rig out onto the road, he jumped out.

"Lista!" Ready!

"Tienes hambre?" Another Mexican held up a piece of meat and waved it at his friend.

The three men at the truck joined the others.

She stared at the open cab door, mesmerized by the silver glimmer of keys in the ignition. Then she began to shake. Jeff and North were in there. She had to save them.

Without even thinking, she pulled out North's revolver and ran for it.

She was inside the cab when the soldiers began to shout. The truck's steering wheel was too big, too heavy. So was the stick shift. She had to sit on the very edge of the hard seat to reach the pedals.

There was a crash of breaking glass inches from her face when she turned the key and started the big engine.

"Don't shoot!" she screamed, fastening her seat belt. *"Soy dama! Tengo miedo!"*

More bullets. She jumped back when she felt a sharp pain in her shoulder. It wasn't a bullet. It was only a shard.

But she got so mad, she aimed the revolver and fired. Then she headed the big eighteen-wheeler straight at them. There was a paper cup and a pint bottle of tequila on the seat beside her. As the truck banged and rattled along the road, the transmission screaming, probably because she was in the wrong gear, she opened the bottle and gulped down fiery bursts of tequila that were so hot she gagged.

She wiped her mouth. In her rearview mirror she could see the Mexicans climbing into the other truck.

She was picking up speed when North spoke sharply from behind her. "Melody! You've got to turn this baby around. Texas is the other way."

"You're okay?"

"I said—"

"Too bad you got your gag off."

"Turn this baby around, damn it!"

"But there's a fence—"

"Drive over it!"

A funny kind of smile lit her face. "I've always wanted

to do something like this! And I thought ranch life was boring!''

She bounced them over rocks and cacti. By the time she had the rig back on the road heading the right way, the other cattle truck was heading straight at her, swerving into her lane deliberately.

''Damn 'em. Veer off the road or we'll lose both trucks,'' North yelled.

''You're not in charge here, Rancher Black! I am!''

Melody took another pull from the tequila bottle and aimed right at them.

''Damn your crazy hide!''

The two embattled cattle trucks met in a cloud of dark boiling dust. The other trunk honked and honked maniacally.

''This is suicide!'' North screamed.

Melody stomped down harder on the accelerator. Only at the last moment did she swerve, and then just a little. So did they.

It was enough. The cabs missed by inches. Only the cattle trailers scraped, making huge rending sounds like giant can openers peeling off lids. The cattle bawled and stomped.

Then she was free. She hit the horn triumphantly and kept tooting it until she saw their headlights in her rearview mirror again.

She cursed.

They'd turned around and were catching up fast.

North was swearing louder than she was when the bandits pulled alongside her and began screaming at her in Spanish, honking and then ramming her. Then just as the thick-shouldered man in the passenger seat pointed a rifle at her face, she saw a clear track off to the right of the roadbed about eight feet below her.

She downshifted and spilled tequila all over her jeans.

''Oops!''

Above his white gag, Jeff's eyes were as big as blue

soccer balls. Right before she skidded the rig off the embankment, she crossed herself. Then she took a final swig
from the nearly empty tequila bottle.

They were bouncing over rocks again and sliding, the
trailer fishtailing all the way down the embankment. The
cab careened to one side wildly. Somehow, miraculously,
they were upright when the front tires hit the lower track.

She floored the accelerator. Above them, the other cattle
truck downshifted, attempting to outrun her as they raced
for the border.

Jeff's gag had slipped. He began to smile as she got
ahead of the other truck. "She's beatin' 'em."

"How the hell does she intend to get back up on the
road?" North demanded.

As if in answer the big truck shuddered as she ran it off
a high bank into a dry riverbed.

When Melody saw water and shingly river rocks, she
began to pray and cross herself.

"We're in the Rio Grande!" North screamed.

Suddenly, up ahead, she saw a ramp where she could get
the truck up onto a low water bridge. But there was some
sort of fence across the middle of the bridge on the higher
road, and the other cattle truck was gaining on her again.

Behind her she heard the spray of gunfire. Then she
crashed onto the bridge and sent fence stakes and barbed
wire flying as she hurdled through the makeshift fence.

"Good Old Ameri-kee! We're home! Now all we have
to do is wait for Delfino to show up." Jeff was babbling
excitedly about the Border Patrol being on their way because he'd called them right after he'd called North when
she crashed into a mesquite tree.

The other truck roared to a stop behind her and twelve
men surrounded the rig with raised guns. She lifted her
hands, surrendering.

A man with dark black hair and mustache swaggered up
to the truck and yanked the door open. As he stood beneath
her, she knew he had to be the Midnight Bandit.

His expensive shirt was tight across his shoulders, tight across his waist, which had thickened some in middle age. Although he was past his first youth, he was still very attractive as only a vital, dangerous man can be.

"Take off your mirrored glasses," she called down to him.

When he did so and then offered her his hand, she noticed his heavy gold watch that had thick links the size and shape of small bulldozer tracks.

"So, are you the famous bandit I've heard so much about?"

"Three things make the heart beat fast, *señorita*—money, danger and a beautiful woman."

Twelve men stood behind him.

This time North was tied up and couldn't save her.

But what could they do to her, even if there were twelve, that the four boys hadn't already done on that long-ago afternoon? Strangely, when she jumped down, she realized her old fears were gone.

This man and his outlaw gang couldn't scare her.

Unless she let him.

"Let North Black and his foreman go," she said.

The Midnight Bandit laughed. "Beautiful and brave, too? Señor Black is luckier than I knew." He paused, tweaking his mustache. "We will go back to Mexico, you and me, and I will build you a fire and roast another cow, and I will think about it. It has been a long time since I dined by candlelight with a very beautiful, a very special woman. The way you drove that truck! Wow!—as you gringos say! You are *muy macha*. Tonight I will show you the real Mexico."

He had her hand in his and was shouting to his men to drive her truck back over the bridge when—

Whoomph! *Zoom!*

"Qué es eso—"

The roar of ten Dodge Ramchargers, their lights blazing sent twelve bandits, even Melody's new admirer, the Midnight Bandit, scampering into the thick mesquite or wading back across the river.

"You're late, Delfino," North said as he rubbed the red places on his wrist that had been bound. He was drinking water out of a paper cup.

"What's going on here?" Delfino demanded.

"Those bastards were trying to take my trucks into Mexico again. They were going to hold Jeff for ransom."

"Fence is down on the low water—"

"They cut it."

Delfino leaned behind North and peeled barbed wire off the bumper of the truck Melody had just driven across the river. "How come your tires are wet?"

Both men eyed each other warily. "There's more to this than meets the eye, I reckon," Delfino said. But he smiled.

"Thanks for showing up, Delfino. You damn sure saved the day."

For the first time since North had gotten out of the truck, Melody dared to look at him.

Fury harshened his features as his gaze locked on her pale face. "You sure made a fool of me."

"I-is that all that counts? I—I thought I saved your life."

He crushed his cup and threw it to the ground.

His black eyes were dead even before he turned his back on her and walked off with Delfino.

Although she sat beside North as he drove back to the ranch headquarters, he neither looked at her nor said a single word to her.

Fourteen

North drove the truck home so fast, Melody felt as if she was in a giant eggbeater that was literally pounding her to death over the rough potholes. W.T. and Arturo had been sent to get the other truck.

Straining to see ahead in the flying darkness, North leaned over the steering wheel. His huge body was rigid and silent; his hand was like a claw on the stick shift.

She didn't think she'd ever been in the presence of such raw, naked hostility.

He banged the truck over a cattle guard, and she gasped in anxious relief at the sight of the lights gleaming cheerily from the big house.

North slammed on the brakes, and she was thrown against her seat belt and him when the rig careened to a stop.

"Whoa! I don't know which was scarier—your driving or her partyin' with the Midnight Bandit. Or the way you're acting now."

With a frown Jeff stared at North's belligerent profile and then at the barn. ''Didn't think I'd ever see any of this again.'' He regarded North's dark silent face uneasily. Then he grabbed an armful of shotguns.

''Time to go, huh?'' Pulling up the door lock, Jeff scooted his large bulk forward, fumbling with the latch to let himself out.

''You were great, Mel,'' Jeff whispered, patting her shoulder. ''Thanks.'' The gratitude in his blue eyes made her forgive him everything.

''Thanks,'' she whispered.

''Better not to talk to him till he has a good night's sleep,'' Jeff said.

North bristled but said nothing until Melody began to slide across her seat after Jeff.

Then North grabbed her hand, wrenching her back. ''You're not going anywhere! Not till we talk!'' The command cracked like a bullet.

Startled, she hesitated before daring a glance at him. The dark sensuality of his brutal features made her catch her breath. Then every wary nerve in her body sparked in painful defiance.

Only a few hours ago, he'd been in her bed—been inside her. And she'd loved it, really loved it.

She loved him.

''North,'' she breathed. ''I'm sorry.''

''So the hell am I. That's why we settle up now. The sooner I'm done with you the better—''

''Done? How bleak that sounds.''

His white face was blank; his black eyes glittered. She began to tremble even before full understanding of what he meant registered.

''As soon as this Aunt Irma, or whoever she is, gets here today, I want you gone. Off my ranch. Out of my life.''

Her skin felt hot and cold at the same time.

''You can't mean…'' Her heart pumped painfully.

He didn't reply.

He was killing her first with words, now with his silence.

"But I saved your life—"

"Do you want a medal? Do you want me down on my knees licking your hand the way you had Jeff—"

His harsh words were like blows. All of a sudden she hurt all over. "No…"

She sucked in a breath as panic raced through her.

"This is my ranch." His voice was tight and angry. "Everybody who sets foot on my land is my responsibility—including you. You deliberately disobeyed me."

"So, that's it. This is about your stupid macho pride."

A hard blue vein throbbed in his temple. "You made a fool of me."

"You're mad because I saved you. Because you didn't protect me."

His lips were pale with leashed rage.

"Where is it written you're the only person in the universe who can be a hero?"

"Don't give yourself airs!"

"You said you wanted a real woman. Well, we had sex, and I loved it so much I want to do it again and again." She remembered how rosy she'd felt, how warm and sweet when she'd ached for him afterward. "Because… Because I love you with all my heart."

"I don't give a damn about that! It was just physical. Something I could get with any woman."

With three cruel sentences he obliterated the warm, sweet rosy memory that had kept her fighting for him, for them, all night.

Something I could get with any woman.

Her body felt as if it were closing down, shriveling up.

Still, she wasn't about to back down.

"Well, if you wanted me to be your woman in that way, even if it doesn't mean as much to you as it did to me, I *was* your woman. Like you said, no matter what happens, we'll have that time together in bed…in our hearts and our minds. Nothing you can say now can take that away—from either of us.'' She paused. "But something else happened to me tonight. Something more wonderful even than the sex we shared. I lost my fear. I won't ever be that child those boys chased and you saved. I'm past all that. Because of tonight and you, I can move forward in my life. Even if…if I lose you, I won't lose that.''

"You're as crazy as you ever were.''

"You were in danger. I saved your life. And Jeff's. And your trucks. And your precious cows.''

"Don't forget—you even flirted with that monster while he had me trussed like a pig for his spit.''

"That, too. I beat him at your game. And I needed to know I could do something like that…at least once in my life. I'm sorry if you can't forgive me, but I had to do it for you…and for me.'' She hesitated. "When they took you, I would have done anything…*anything*…to save your life, North. You are that precious to me. And no matter what you say or do to me, I would rather have you hate me now than have you dead in Mexico.''

"I want that kid who's upstairs in my father's room gone by tonight, and I want you gone, too, do you understand?''

She'd become his woman.

She'd saved his life.

She'd come into her own power.

But in doing so, she'd lost him.

Melody was sitting cross-legged on a little blanket she'd thrown down in the llamas' stall. Little Camel stood beside her sucking vigorously on the bottle's nipple.

"Why won't his mother feed him?'' Teo whispered. "Doesn't his mother like him? If she wasn't locked up, would she run away?''

"Her milk won't come.''

In the next breath he demanded, "When will Aunt Irma get here?''

Even with black hair clean and gleaming, even in the brand-new plaid cowboy shirt, jeans and new boots that

North had bought him, even after he'd grabbed a huge breakfast, Teo still looked the waif. He was a quiet, self-controlled little boy. He had a deep, natural reserve. He was even shyer than Little Camel.

"Soon I think," Melody reassured him. "It is a six-hour drive from Houston."

The mother llama seemed to be taking an inordinate interest in her baby sucking at that nipple. All of a sudden she walked over and began pawing straw and then nuzzling her baby.

Little Camel stopped sucking.

"Teo watch—"

The child held his breath as Little Camel cautiously stuck his head under her belly and began to suckle.

"Oh," Melody gasped, setting the bottle down. "Aren't they cute?"

Teo smiled for the first time since Melody had met him. She pulled the little boy into her arms where he stayed until the barn doors rolled apart. He jumped when heavy boot heels clacked briskly toward them on concrete.

"Melody—"

"North?"

They hadn't spoken since they'd gotten out of the truck. After all, what was there to say?

"In here," she called.

The door opened, and her gaze climbed long legs encased in pressed denim. Just his nearness gave her a physical ache. It seemed forever since he'd held her and kissed her, since his black eyes had gleamed with hungry desire.

He was bronzed in his white shirt and jeans, as lean and handsome as ever, maybe more so since she'd lost him. Maybe more so, since she'd *had* him.

There were shadows under his eyes, and his expression was worn and sad. His beautiful mouth was thin. He wore the look of a man who'd lost his dreams.

She wanted to tell him that it didn't have to be that way. Instead she pressed her fingertips to her lips. He was as stubborn as she was. There were some things a person had to decide for himself. He'd made up his mind.

"Look who's here, Teo," he said, ignoring Melody as he pushed the door wider.

"Teo. *Precioso*," said a soft feminine voice in Spanish behind North.

Straw crunched as a small brown woman in a black dress and shawl knelt and held out her arms.

"*Tiá?*"

When Melody gave him a little push Teo walked hesitantly up to the older woman with the kind wrinkled face.

"*Sí, precioso. Tu Tiá* Irma." She wrapped him in her arms and held him for a long time. Finally she got up, and leading Teo by the hand, North and Melody followed them outside to the battered car she'd borrowed from her cousin.

Arm in arm, Manolete and Sissy joined them. His eyes wet and shining, Manolete knelt and hugged Teo for a very long time.

"I'm a cook," Irma explained. "I'll take good care of him."

"I know you will," said Manolete, releasing Teo, so the boy and Irma could get inside the car.

"You be good, Teo, you hear," Melody said.

"Take care of Little Camel," he replied.

"He has his mother. He doesn't need me anymore." Melody wasn't looking at Teo, though. She was staring at North who stood next to her.

Then to North the little boy said in a small timid voice, "Can I come back for a visit? I'm real good with animals. I worked on a rancho. I could feed all your sick babies. I can milk the cows—I—I can even feed camels."

Irma laughed.

North reached inside and patted the child's glossy black head. "Anytime. Always. *Mi casa es su casa.*"

North leaned down. To Irma, in English, he said, "If you need any help getting him papers, I know people on both sides of the border."

Irma smiled. "You are a very powerful man. A true hero to save this little boy."

North stood up, his face grim. "I'm no hero. Thank these other people."

Irma started the car. Black smoke belched.

Wrapped in each other's arms, Manolete and Sissy seemed very much in love as they waved goodbye.

Melody felt chilled standing so close to North, both of them waving and smiling until the car vanished behind a wall of thick brush. Then their eyes locked, and North's smile died.

A feeling of apprehension washed through Melody. "I guess it's my turn to say goodbye."

"Don't bother," North muttered flatly, his hard gaze flicking away from Melody before he pivoted and walked away.

Melody felt sick.

"He loves you," Sissy whispered. "He does. And it's killing him. I'm his sister. I know." Then she looked up at Manolete. "Mano leaves me, too, today."

"Really?" Melody could barely concentrate on anything other than North's tall form striding away. "North wrote letters of introduction to all our rancher friends, so Mano will have places to stay on the way to New York. This morning I bought my ticket. I'll be there waiting when he gets there."

"Oh, Sissy."

"We shall see what the future will bring," Manolete said.

He took Sissy in his arms and kissed her full on the lips.

"I'm so happy for you," Melody whispered.

Melody was staring at the awful landscapes in his office. North was seated at his desk shuffling papers.

"North—"

He wouldn't look at her.

"Why won't you listen to me?" she begged.

He wadded a paper and pitched it into the trash. "We already discussed this. You could have died. It would have been my fault. I can't risk that again."

"I saved your life. And I'm not sorry I did. I can't play by your rules all the time. I have to be me. I have to take care of me, too. And sometimes I may have to take care of you, too."

"You could have died."

"That's not a crime. You only think it is be-cause…because of the way your daddy died."

He slammed a file closed.

"You didn't kill him."

"Who said I did?"

"Nobody."

"Then why'd you accuse—"

"You accuse yourself. Nobody else accuses you. Why do you do that? Why can't you let it go?"

He stood up. "You want to know why? If I tell you you'll go—"

She nodded, backing into the hall.

"I was twelve. My daddy smoked, and I wanted to do everything he did. So Jeff and me, we were out behind some stacks of lumber with a package of his cigarettes I'd stolen out of his room. We only smoked one, but we both got so sick. We were throwing up our gizzards in the house when the fire started. Hell, nobody knows how it got started. But all of a sudden this black smoke was billowing so high every neighbor in three counties drove up to see what was the matter."

The dark torment in his eyes crushed her. She knew what it was to love one's family, to want to take care of them.

"I—I wish there was something I could say…do…"

"Little Miss Fix-it! You think this is like some cut you can put a Band-Aid on and make it well. You think you're magic after what you did last night—"

"No."

"You think I'm some worthless, cowardly incompetent

because the Midnight Bandit got the best of me and you
came to my rescue.''

''No, North. I just think you're human.''

''Get out.''

In a quiet voice, she said, ''I love you.''

''I love you, too. Get the hell out!''

Fifteen

A big engine outside the barn roared to life.

"What the hell was that?" North muttered, wiping his brow in his shirtsleeve. The relentless drought persisted endlessly. So did the summer. Even though it was still early that morning, North and Jeff were already sweating in the barn as they jotted notes on their clipboards as they went over the day's work together.

"That's W.T. I told him to put the truck on bungee autopilot while he feeds hay in the north pasture," Jeff said.

"Hell! I just put Little Camel and his mother in that pasture!"

North threw his clipboard down. He was already yelling to W.T. to cut the engine as he ran out of the barn.

But W.T. couldn't hear him over the noise of the truck. Instead of watching what he was doing, the rangy, no-good cowboy was lying down in the cab, his Stetson tipped low over his nose, reading a comic book.

Behind the huge truck, Little Camel was cornered.

At the exact moment Little Camel saw North and might have bolted clear, the steel bumper hit the little animal and knocked him down.

"Get up!" North yelled. "W.T.," he screamed.

As the big wheels rolled closer to the fallen animal, Little Camel just lay there, too stunned to move.

Then the truck ground its gears and lurched backward.

North leaped over the fence. "Get up! Get out of the way!"

Little Camel lifted his head. As he looked at North he seemed to understand and made a valiant struggle to stand. He was halfway to his feet when the truck knocked him down and backed over him. The llama's legs twisted and jerked under the big black double wheels. Then he disappeared completely.

"No! No!"

W.T. finally heard North banging on the door and stopped the truck. He jumped out, his comic book still rolled up in his hand. North shoved past him, hopped inside the cab and put the gear in first.

When he'd gotten the truck off the animal, he jumped out and ran back to Little Camel. But the llama was a still and broken thing in the deep soil. After his mother came up and got her fill of sniffing and licking his nose, North knelt and lifted the frail, furry body into his arms.

Before North reached the barn with his pet, Gran had come running out of the house. Jeff and Sissy were there, too.

Nobody spoke as the hot wind gusted around the house.

"Why don't you bury him under my daisies," Gran offered after a lengthy silent interval. "That's the prettiest spot on the ranch. I'm going to get W.T. to plant me some tulips come spring."

"I'll get the shovel for you," Jeff offered.

There were tears in North's eyes as he dug the small grave.

"Could I take a turn...on the shovel?" W.T. finally whispered.

North turned, his heart dark and blank until he read the bleak despair in the boy's expression and saw the sheen of tears in his eyes.

He swallowed. After a long moment he nodded. "It was an accident. It was just an accident."

North stayed by the grave long after the others had gone.

He thought of his father, of Melody, and the memories of the people he'd loved and lost made him ache.

As he stared at Little Camel's grave, the loneliness he'd thought he could accept suddenly threatened to overwhelm him. The thought of eating alone, of going to bed alone, of waking up every day for the rest of his life without Melody nestled warmly against him brought unbearable pain.

But when he thought of his father and the fire, the ghosts from his past were too real.

What he'd done to his father was too real.

Little Camel's death was a reminder.

He couldn't risk Melody.

It had been a rough month. Not just for North. For everybody on the ranch who had dealings with North.

"Calf breathing okay?"

"Yeah, King," Jeff replied glumly.

North frowned as he dropped more antibiotics into the uterus and then began to sew up the cow. It had been a rough delivery. He'd slipped and the cow had stomped him mighty hard in a lot of tender places a man didn't care to catch a hoof.

"You know, King—"

North could tell by the level of gravel in Jeff's tone what he was up to again, so he cut him off at the pass. "I don't want to talk about *her*."

"You don't look so good. You're back to killing yourself with work again."

"I'm fine."

"You fell. You damn near got you and me both killed. You aren't some god."

"Never said I was."

"You can make a mistake, too."

"I know that! Don't you think I know that?"

"I was wrong about her, King."

"I said don't."

"So are you. You've been wrong about a lot of things. About your daddy—"

"Damn it."

"She didn't show you up. She was safe. You protected her. You faced those guys alone. Give her credit for having the guts to come back for you. She saved our lives, our cattle and our trucks."

"I know what she did better than you!"

"Give yourself credit for saving her. But, hell, she's the best damn cowhand on the place. We need her. Not just for that. But because you're dying on the inside, North. You're so damn proud and stubborn, you're killing yourself just like you did after Rand died. Everything's not your fault, you know. Little Camel's death was an accident, just like your daddy's. You forgave W.T. Why the hell can't you forgive yourself?"

"It's not the same thing."

"You need her. The ranch needs her. So—go get her."

"Hell, she wouldn't have me, and I wouldn't blame her. So, forget it."

"Track her down, throw her over your shoulder and show her she belongs with you—here."

"This ain't the Wild West anymore."

"You could've damn sure fooled me the night she outrustled the Midnight Bandit. Why don't you get off your high horse and go get her?"

North frowned as he remembered what she'd said that haunted him every night when he tried to sleep.

You said you wanted a real woman. Well, we had sex, and I loved it so much I want to do it again and again.

And what had he said? He'd lied and said what they'd had he could get with any other woman.

She'd looked so sad, so hurt.

But she'd fought for their love anyway. She'd stood up to him, arguing that he was wrong, that she had a right to be a whole person, too.

She'd saved his life.

"Just because she's a hero doesn't mean you aren't one, too, King. You two are cut out of the same cloth. She's worthy of you, worthy of El Dorado. Don't do something real stupid by being so damn stubborn."

Slowly, as North remembered first the wild sex and then their adventure, his eyes lit up from the inside out.

Jeff read him and smiled. "That's the ticket."

"She sure was something, wasn't she?" North said slowly. "The way she drove the truck. Hell, she couldn't even reach the pedals."

"Go get her, why dontcha?" Jeff whispered.

"It's gonna take a lot of nerve."

"The lady's a hero. The question is do you have as much nerve and heart and gumption as that little gal does?"

"Will you marry—"

North was in the shower trying to work up his nerve. He'd called her, but she hadn't answered. So, he'd left a tongue-tied message on her machine that said he wanted to see her.

Then he'd gone straight to Kingsville and stopped at the first jewelry store he'd come to. Hell, when all the salesgirls had surrounded him, he'd been like a shy teenager.

The manager had beamed when North had said, "I want to see your diamond rings."

"For an engagement ring, Mr. Black?"

North had lowered his Stetson over his face and nodded.

"She must be very special?"

"You've got that right."

"Unique."

North had tipped his Stetson back. "You wouldn't be-lieve—"

The manager had known who he was, right off. Hell, everybody knew who he was. So, he'd pulled out a tray of huge diamonds.

"You don't understand," North had drawled. "I want the smallest diamond you've got."

"But if she's so special—"

"Like I said, you don't understand—I didn't, either, for an awfully long time."

The memory made him frown. When North turned off the water, the bathroom was full of steam. The tiny room, like his house, like the ranch, felt so empty without Melody.

He opened the shower door to reach for his towel.

But the girl he'd dreamed of night and day was there, wearing a black lace bra and thong underwear.

"Do you want to dance?" Melody whispered in her sexy voice as she began to hum their song.

"What are you doing here?"

"You called, Bertie Boy." She snapped her fingers. "I came." She threw back her head and laughed nervously. "I'm afraid I'm playing easy to get."

"It took you long enough."

"You can be pretty stubborn, too, Bertie."

"We're a matched pair."

"I certainly hope so." She hesitated. "I was in class. I called home for my messages.... I—I listened to yours over and over. Then I called the ranch and Sissy said you'd gone into Kingsville to buy me a ring."

"Sissy told you that?"

"She said you would be back before I could drive here. So I hopped in my car...and I flew so fast I couldn't even read bumper stickers."

"We're going to have to talk about your driving...about what you did to my truck..."

"Not for a while...." She stepped forward and pushed

him back against the steaming wall. "You've got some hoofprints in lots of interesting places."

"Some people around here have been telling me I've been on a self-destructive tear," he admitted roughly, running his hand through her long hair.

"I wonder why?"

"'Cause I was hell-bent not to see the obvious." He kissed her throat.

"Don't you think it's time we finished what we started?" she murmured. "You promised, remember?"

"Way past time," he agreed when she peeled off her panties and tossed them on top of the neat pile of clothes he'd stacked to put on after his shower.

He picked her up, and she circled him with her legs. Suddenly just holding her sent flashes of fire sizzling all through him.

"Oh, Bertie," she moaned softly.

"You're going to marry me this time, aren't you?" he whispered. "'Cause I bought you a ring with the smallest diamond you ever saw."

"Really?"

"It's microscopic."

She laughed throatily. "I don't think I can go through the white dress routine again or people like the governor coming to watch us get married."

"Neither can I."

"Oh, Bertie. I hurt you…when I ran away on our wedding day."

"And I hurt you when I was so pigheaded I sent you away after you saved me and Jeff and my cows."

"So, maybe that means it's time for happily ever after?"

"Sounds like a winner," North murmured.

He kissed her as if he were starving for her. She met his kisses with a response that was needy and hot.

They made love, first against the bathroom wall, and then in his bed. And everything they did was exciting and wonderful and absolutely perfect.

If he was wild, she was equally so, and after it was over, he held her in his arms and felt happier than he had ever felt before—even when his father had been alive. It was as if at last, with her at his side, he was complete.

He didn't have to control her. He had to believe in her, to let her be, to trust her. And now that she knew who she was, she didn't have to be afraid of anything—not of sex, not of him, not of their life together. She could teach. She could live at the ranch. She could choose. She was his woman. But she was her own woman, too.

"Show me the ring," she whispered a little breathlessly.

He pulled out a black velvet box.

The ring fit her slender finger perfectly.

"Turn on the light so I can see the diamond."

He did so.

"Oh, Bertie, I think you got a little carried away. I need a magnifying glass."

He took a quick, worried breath.

"But I love it. It's me. Mrs. Rancher Black. What do you say we run down to Mexico tonight—and get married."

He laughed. He felt young and happy. "This time, I'll drive, Mrs. Rancher Black."

*   *   *   *   *

*Look for another one of
Ann Major's exciting titles
from MIRA Books
in the fall of 2002!*

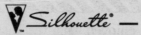

Feel like a star with Silhouette.

We will fly you and a guest to New York City for an exciting weekend stay at a glamorous 5-star hotel. Experience a refreshing day at one of New York's trendiest spas and have your photo taken by a professional. Plus, receive $1,000 U.S. spending money!

**Flowers...long walks...dinner for two...
how does Silhouette Books
make romance come alive for you?**

Send us a script, with 500 words or less, along with visuals (only drawings, magazine cutouts or photographs or combination thereof). Show us how Silhouette Makes Your Love Come Alive. Be creative and have fun. No purchase necessary. All entries must be clearly marked with your name, address and telephone number. All entries will become property of Silhouette and are not returnable. **Contest closes September 28, 2001.**

Please send your entry to: **Silhouette Makes You a Star!**

In U.S.A.	In Canada
P.O. Box 9069	P.O. Box 637
Buffalo, NY, 14269-9069	Fort Erie, ON, L2A 5X3

Look for contest details on the next page, by visiting www.eHarlequin.com or request a copy by sending a self-addressed envelope to the applicable address above. Contest open to Canadian and U.S. residents who are 18 or over. Void where prohibited.

Our lucky winner's photo will appear in a Silhouette ad. Join the fun!

HARLEQUIN "SILHOUETTE MAKES YOU A STAR!" CONTEST 1308
OFFICIAL RULES
NO PURCHASE NECESSARY TO ENTER

1. To enter, follow directions published in the offer to which you are responding. Contest begins June 1, 2001, and ends on September 28, 2001. Entries must be postmarked by September 28, 2001, and received by October 5, 2001. Enter by hand-printing (or typing) on an 8 ½" x 11" piece of paper your name, address (including zip code), contest number/name and attaching a script containing <u>500 words</u> or less, <u>along with drawings, photographs or magazine cutouts, or combinations thereof</u> (i.e., collage) on no larger than 9" x 12" piece of paper, describing how the <u>Silhouette books make romance come alive for you.</u> Mail via first-class mail to: Harlequin "Silhouette Makes You a Star!" Contest 1308, (in the U.S.) P.O. Box 9069, Buffalo, NY 14269-9069, (in Canada) P.O. Box 637, Fort Erie, Ontario, Canada L2A 5X3. Limit one entry per person, household or organization.

2. Contests will be judged by a panel of members of the Harlequin editorial, marketing and public relations staff. Fifty percent of criteria will be judged against script and fifty percent will be judged against drawing, photographs and/or magazine cutouts. Judging criteria will be based on the following:

   - Sincerity—25%
   - Originality and Creativity—50%
   - Emotionally Compelling—25%

   In the event of a tie, duplicate prizes will be awarded. Decisions of the judges are final.

3. All entries become the property of Torstar Corp. and may be used for future promotional purposes. Entries will not be returned. No responsibility is assumed for lost, late, illegible, incomplete, inaccurate, nondelivered or misdirected mail.

4. Contest open only to residents of the U.S. <u>(except Puerto Rico)</u> and Canada who are 18 years of age or older, and is void wherever prohibited by law; all applicable laws and regulations apply. Any litigation within the Province of Quebec respecting the conduct or organization of a publicity contest may be submitted to the Régie des alcools, des courses et des jeux for a ruling. Any litigation respecting the awarding of a prize may be submitted to the Régie des alcools, des courses et des jeux only for the purpose of helping the parties reach a settlement. Employees and immediate family members of Torstar Corp. and D. L. Blair, Inc., their affiliates, subsidiaries and all other agencies, entities and persons connected with the use, marketing or conduct of this contest are not eligible to enter. Taxes on prizes are the sole responsibility of the winner. Acceptance of any prize offered constitutes permission to use winner's name, photograph or other likeness for the purposes of advertising, trade and promotion on behalf of Torstar Corp., its affiliates and subsidiaries without further compensation to the winner, unless prohibited by law.

5. Winner will be determined no later than November 30, 2001, and will be notified by mail. Winner will be required to sign and return an Affidavit of Eligibility/Release of Liability/Publicity Release form within 15 days after winner notification. Noncompliance within that time period may result in disqualification and an alternative winner may be selected. All travelers must execute a Release of Liability prior to ticketing and must possess required travel documents (e.g., passport, photo ID) where applicable. Trip must be booked by December 31, 2001, and completed within one year of notification. No substitution of prize permitted by winner. Torstar Corp. and D. L. Blair, Inc., their parents, affiliates and subsidiaries are not responsible for errors in printing of contest, entries and/or game pieces. In the event of printing or other errors that may result in unintended prize values or duplication of prizes, all affected game pieces or entries shall be null and void. **Purchase or acceptance of a product offer does not improve your chances of winning.**

6. Prizes: (1) Grand Prize—A 2-night/3-day trip for two (2) to New York City, including round-trip coach air transportation nearest winner's home and hotel accommodations (double occupancy) at The Plaza Hotel, a glamorous afternoon makeover at <u>a trendy New York spa,</u> $1,000 in U.S. spending money and an opportunity to <u>have a professional photo taken and appear in a Silhouette advertisement</u> (approximate retail value: $7,000). (10) Ten Runner-Up Prizes of gift packages (retail value $50 ea.). Prizes consist of only those items listed as part of the prize. Limit one prize per person. Prize is valued in U.S. currency.

7. For the name of the winner (available after December 31, 2001) send a self-addressed, stamped envelope to: Harlequin "Silhouette Makes You a Star!" Contest 1197 Winners, P.O. Box 4200 Blair, NE 68009-4200 or you may access the www.eHarlequin.com Web site through February 28, 2002.

Contest sponsored by Torstar Corp., P.O Box 9042, Buffalo, NY 14269-9042.

COMING NEXT MONTH

#1381 HARD TO FORGET—Annette Broadrick
Man of the Month
Although Joe Sanchez hadn't seen Elena Moldonado in over ten years, he'd never forgotten his high school sweetheart. Now that Elena was back in town, Joe wanted her back in *his* arms. The stormy passion between them proved as wild as ever, but Joe would have to regain Elena's trust before he'd have a chance at the love of a lifetime.

#1382 A LOVING MAN—Cait London
Rose Granger didn't want to have a thing to do with worldly and sophisticated Stefan Donatien! She preferred her life just as it was, without the risk of heartbreak. Besides, what could the handsome Stefan possibly see in a simple small-town woman? But Stefan's tender seductions were irresistible, and Rose found herself wishing he would stay…forever.

#1383 HAVING HIS CHILD—Amy J. Fetzer
Wife, Inc./The Baby Bank
With no husband in sight and her biological clock ticking, Angela Justice figured the local sperm bank was the only way to make her dreams of having a baby come true. That was before Angela's best friend, Dr. Lucas Ryder, discovered her plans and decided to grant her wish—the old-fashioned way!

#1384 BABY OF FORTUNE—Shirley Rogers
Fortunes of Texas: The Lost Heirs
Upon discovering that he was an heir to the famed Fortune clan, Justin Bond resolved to give his marriage a second chance. His estranged wife, Heather, was more than willing to welcome Justin back into her life. But would Justin welcome Heather back into his heart when he learned the secret his wife had kept from him?

#1385 UNDERCOVER SULTAN—Alexandra Sellers
Sons of the Desert: The Sultans
When corporate spy Mariel de Vouvray was forced into an uneasy partnership with Sheikh Haroun al Jawadi, her powerful attraction to him didn't make things any easier! With every new adventure, Mariel fell further under the spell of her seductive sheikh, and soon she longed to make their partnership into something far more permanent.

#1386 BEAUTY IN HIS BEDROOM—Ashley Summers
Clint Whitfield came home after two years overseas and found feisty Regina Flynn living in his mansion. His first instinct was to throw the lovely strawberry blond intruder off his property—and out of his life. His second instinct was to let her stay—and to persuade the delectable Gina *into* his bedroom!

SDCNM0701